I STAND CORRECTED

PATRICIA ASEDEGBEGA NIETO

This book is dedicated to Daniel, Esther and John Joseph.
Sobran las palabras ☺

ONE

BALOU

They say that in order to leave your mark in this world, you have to plant a tree, bear a son and write a book. Well I have been neutered, I dig out more than dig in, so all I can do dear readers to attain some form of immortality is to share my story with you all. I do have to warn you that my version of all that occurred is only for those that have a vivid imagination. If you are going to pick up this book and utter an exclamation of "Cats can´t do that", then you really don´t know a lot about cats and if you allow me to make a suggestion... it´s best you put the book down and read the newspaper or something similar.

Let me introduce myself, so you can start forming an idea about the main character in the events that are about to unfold before your eyes as you turn the pages of this book. My name is Balou and I come from the fine and noble breed of the British Shorthair. Now, there are cats everywhere you look, different breeds, sizes, colours, temperament... But we all have one thing in common; we all firmly believe that man was put on this earth for the sole purpose of catering to our needs. When you hear it said that cats tend to look at you with disdain, it is because we feel we are doing you a favour by setting our eyes on you. I am as black as soot and regarding my general appearance, some might in ignorance, label me as fat, but I´m actually what the enlightened would call big-boned and of a stout constitution. This coupled with my soft silky fur makes people compare me to a teddy bear; the most arresting thing about my appearance are my big eyes, bright yellow or orange depending on the occasion, they go very well with the colour of my fur. As humility is not one of my many virtues, I can say without turning a hair or blinking an eye that you shall never find a better looking specimen than me; you can try, but everyone can´t be in the wrong except you and besides, it´s something I´m being told constantly.

    The earliest memory that comes to my mind is one in which I´m playing with my brothers under the ever vigilant stare of our mother; she was always ready to intervene in case we got carried away and played too roughly. She wasn't one to fear taking a swipe at us with her paw to keep us in check. I still remember the way she would hold us down tightly while she groomed us with her raspy tongue as we desperately struggled for our freedom, one by one each of us endured this inevitable form of torture that she seemed to enjoy indulging in, all too often. If I am a clean cat today, it's because my mother made sure we understood the importance of a good grooming session, every part of our body was included in this regime, she took her time and made sure of that. To this day, it is a routine no one can distract me from as it is an exercise that requires my full attention. I have to say, I learnt from the best.

I think as far as kittens go we were extremely happy, everything was a toy to play with or prey to hunt, especially the feet of the very tall and strange creatures we lived with. We had so much fun pouncing on them, they were never fast enough getting out-of-the-way and we would sink our tiny teeth into their ankles, they would then hold us by the scruff and shake us while talking to us in a stern voice but we took absolutely no notice and as soon as we were let down, we would rush to attack another pair of legs. When we weren't sleeping, we would take part in such games or hide behind doors and scare the unsuspecting passerby. We were living the dream life of any kitten, we didn't have a care in the world.

Then one day, when we were about eight weeks old, everything changed. On this particular morning, the dominant male of the house, Pedro, came into the room where we were usually locked in for the night, he had with him a cardboard box; he put five of us in the box and closed the lid. It was all so sudden, I didn´t even have time to look at my mother one last time, I did however hear her cry as each one of us was taken from her side. The box had little holes in the sides and we all tried desperately to look through them. But we couldn't see anything as the man had put a cloth over the box so we were in absolute darkness. We felt as if we were being lifted from the ground and then we were placed on what seemed to be a not so steady surface as it felt like everything was moving around us, later in life I would associate this feeling with car trips. We were so scared, we cried until we lost our voices and could meow no more.

Suddenly the rocking movement stopped and we felt our box being lifted up again, the lid was opened and I blinked as I was hit by a blast of light. I looked up to see where we were and saw four pairs of eyes staring down at us.

"I will give you 400 Euros for five of them." You know people prefer dogs to cats in this country, and until you told me about this breed I had never heard of it, so I´m guessing it´s not very common. My customers are used to me bringing in Persians once in a while, but even those are hard to sell as so many cats are on the streets or in shelters these days and they can get them for free if they wanted one."

"400 Euros? You must be joking. Each one of them would cost that amount, Google the breed and you will see how much they are going for. I can´t part with them for that pitiful amount, that´s daylight robbery. They have all had their first vaccinations, been well fed and cared for. I need to be able to show a profit from the sale, no matter how small!" replied Pedro.

"Well you are not a registered breeder, you just mated your cat with the stud that you found advertised online from the same breed but you haven´t done much research or even tested the parents to see if they can be used for such purposes. I´m actually doing you a favour as you probably won´t be able to even find them homes. 400 Euros is my final offer so you can either leave them here or take them and go back the same way you came. Look around you, I have other animals, I can´t spend more than that on cats, you know most people won´t buy a cat when there are so many of them roaming around and living from the waste bins. What do I do with them if I can´t sell them?"

My brothers and I were watching the exchange carefully; we hoped that Pedro would take us back to our mother and not accept the sum that the other man was trying to convince him to take. Finally, we saw him shrug his shoulders and put some money in his wallet. He looked at us once more, patted our heads and left. One by one we were removed from the cardboard box and placed into a larger container, made from glass; the man who had paid for us was busily taping a paper sign to the front of the glass container. The base of the container we had been moved to was full of shredded paper, there was water available and a food bowl the man had filled with dry kibble.

We spent hours crying and hated being in such a small space. Compared to the flat we had been born in, there was hardly any space for us to move about, it was just impossible to chase one another. How did they expect us to play? It wasn't long before we all fell asleep; we were exhausted from the adventures of the day. When I woke up, I lapped some water and looked through the glass frontage of my new surroundings, I could see there were other similar containers to ours and some cages. I took a close look at the one in front of me; it was difficult to see much as it was full of plants. I wondered if there were other kittens like us in there. At first I didn't see anything, but all of a sudden I was startled; there was something crawling slowly in the cage, it looked like the kind of thing I should pounce on and kill, so I readied myself, I calculated the distance and felt that as the other creature had not seen me, the element of surprise was on my side and I would be successful; mother had shown us how to hunt without our prey even noticing us approaching, finally, something exciting was about to take place, I assumed the proper position, crouched down as much as I could to avoid being seen and got ready to jump. That day I learnt a very valuable lesson in life; always make sure there is no glass panel between you and your prey!

Our container was a lively place to be, we were always fighting and playing with the shredded paper when we weren't sleeping on it. At night everyone would leave the store and they would turn off the lights, it became very quiet; the birds, who were our neighbours and spent a great part of the day singing and making noise would finally fall asleep too. They made a horrible racket when they were awake; some of them were so tiny and yet had so much to say. I had hoped someone would just buy them all, especially as I couldn't get at them. It was a constant temptation for us and we spent a lot of hours watching them and fantasising about what we would do if the barriers disappeared. In the morning as soon as the door opened and the lights were switched on, we all came to life; it was an interior shop with no windows leading to the exterior of the building, I really missed feeling the rays of sunlight coming in through the windows. When we lived with Pedro; he who had abandoned us without giving us a second glance, he would let us out onto the terrace every day for a short while, I have to say that the feeling of the warmth of that natural heat on my fur was priceless. Before opening the shop, the owner or his wife would clean and change the paper bed, provide fresh water and fill the food bowl. It was something we all looked forward to as we just shared one bowl; it was soon empty after being filled, as soon as the food touched it, it was gone, they never thought of refilling it, so we were always hungry. During the day, people came in and out of the shop all the time; they stopped and looked in all the containers. The adults brought in the children to keep them entertained for a while; they normally just looked and pointed at the various occupants of the display windows while they read out loud the information pasted on each glass. The little ones were always pointing at one animal or the other and crying because they wanted them. Most of the times they just left the way they came, empty handed but sometimes one lucky animal got to leave the container and go into the wide open space beyond.

We watched the dogs next to us, they appeared to have developed a technique that seemed to be working; they would stand near the glass, making sure they were seen, people kept saying how nice they looked, along with the birds which were often bought, they also got to be a favourite with the daily visitors. Even though it isn´t in our nature to make an effort to be liked, we did try to imitate them and get people to notice us; they did, they would look at us and say how cute we were, the effort paid off. One after the other, each of my four brothers got to leave the glass container. I didn´t understand why I wasn´t picked, I had stood on display with them and even put my adorable little paws on the glass, just like they did. Why hadn't I been chosen I wondered? It wasn't long until I found out why; I overheard the explanation from the shop owner one day...

"We are going to have to lower the price on this one; it seems no one wants him because he is black. Then, if we still can´t sell him, we will need to take him to the shelter, he is taking up valuable space, people only want kittens and the older he gets the less adorable he will become."

I didn´t know what the shelter was, but it seemed I would be on my way there sometime soon; maybe they would be better at finding people who would be interested in taking me out of there. I had even stopped getting up each time someone approached my glass cage. For some reason my colour wasn´t right, so why even bother? I wasn´t going to get picked, what was the use in me trying? When people came over, I continued sleeping, at least I didn´t miss my vital and much needed rest. That was until the day when I sensed that someone was watching me; I just opened one of my eyes and was just about to close it again when something caught my attention...

TWO

ROSARIO

I glance at Javier as we enter the shopping mall. He is in a good mood today, he has decided he wants to get me a belated birthday present and was taking me along to pick what I wanted. Personally I have always felt that presents should be surprises, even if you make a mistake with your choice. The important thing is that you make an effort and just try to find something you think the other person might like; taking someone shopping for their own present is something I find incredibly tacky and tasteless.

As we walk along the corridors of the crowded mall, people turn to look at us, some take photographs with their mobile phones, they don't even bother to hide the fact that they are doing that. I know it will appear in the press the next day; "Rosario and Javier out on a Saturday", everything we do seems to be of interest. We are considered by the public as one of the most glamorous couples on the social scene. People seem to be so interested in the lives of others and there is so much media dedicated to "celebrity" these days due to popular demand. Each time we go out, we find evidence of our outing on the internet or in the weekly society and gossip magazines. Most of the time, the headline attached to the photograph has nothing to do with reality. This has been part of my life for so long that it doesn't bother me anymore.

Javier keeps looking at me as we pass different shops to see if I show interest in anything but nothing catches my eye and I really intend to stick to my guns on this one. I won't be bought; I should have received my gift two months ago! Suddenly, we stop in front of a pet shop and he walks in. I stay outside waiting for him to come back out; the last thing that I want now is an animal, it is a responsibility that I don't feel capable of taking on at the moment. When he comes back, he grabs me by the arm and pulls me inside the shop. There are many animals and birds; the shop also stocks everything they need for their care. Everything anyone could ever need to care for them. Javier leads me to the puppy section; I see that they have different breeds; they even have Golden Retrievers, I´m familiar with those after seeing them in TV adverts. They are cute, but I know I´m not up to the task of committing to daily walks.

"We have seen a lot of shops and you haven´t entered any, so I will decide for you; after all, it is my gift to you. I only brought you along so as not to make a mistake. I think I will buy you a dog, just let me know which one you want."

I glance at him, he has a real look of determination on his face, I know that if I don´t do something quickly, we will be leaving the shop with a dog! I decide to humour him and choose what I think will be the lowest maintenance animal in the shop. The owner had greeted us very warmly when we entered and had followed us closely around his shop. I even saw him discreetly take a photograph with his mobile phone. As soon as he heard my husband´s words he immediately started to try to sell us one of the dogs, he proceeded to tell us about each and every one of them. I look at the animals in their glass cubicles and I feel so sorry for them all, spending their days waiting for someone to show an interest and buy them their freedom.

"It is my present, so I will pick the animal I want and I´m not ready for a dog. Frankly, neither are you as we both spend a lot of hours away from home. As I know that it will be my pet and I will have to take care of it, then it should be my decision."

"That´s fair, take a look around and let me know what you want. I do feel one of these adorable puppies will make a very good companion for you, just look at them, they are so cute!"

I leave him looking at the dogs while the owner rushes after me, he realises the decision lies in my hands and he wants to be the one to sell Rosario Dominguez a pet. He tries to steer me towards the exotic bird area, they have some very attractive specimens and I go with him just out of politeness, but I know that I will be leaving there with a fish.

I smile at him as he takes me from cage to cage, he points out why each bird is better than the previous one. I listen and nod my head at all the appropriate moments. Meanwhile, I have discovered where the fish tanks are and I move towards that area. On the way there, we pass a corridor and I see Javier looking at a glass box, I stop and look too. I'm hoping it´s not a snake, if it were I would have to quickly steer him away, I have a mortal fear of snakes and can't risk going home with one. At that precise moment, a small, round, black kitten opens one of its eyes and then closes it again; it then proceeds to lazily open both eyes and then fixes them on me. He stares at me for a second, as if deciding if I´m worth stretching and getting up for? It seems like he thinks I am because he does just that. Having read the information pasted on the glass frontage of his container I note that he is a male cat. It says he is a British Shorthair; he has yellow eyes, he is completely black and has a round face and a stocky body. I´m not that well versed on cat breeds. I have only seen Siamese and Persian cats before; this breed is new to me. I kneel in front of the container, he comes close to the glass, we just stare at each other, that's when I decide that I won´t be taking a fish home.

"I have never heard of this cat breed, where is it popular? I have not seen it here in Spain before."

"A friend of mine has one of them and I got the litter through him. He is the last one remaining; he came here with his four brothers. Like you, I had never seen this type of cat before, it does seem to be well known in England though."

"How old is he?" I ask.

"He is twelve weeks old now; he is quiet and no trouble at all. He spends most of the day sleeping."

"Javier, this is what I want. So if your offer still stands, this is the birthday present I´ll accept from you."

"I don´t like cats, they are sneaky, sly creatures. Look at the way he is staring at us, like he is doing us a favour by interrupting his sleep and taking time to consider if we are worthy of him. Also, there must be a reason why all his brothers are gone and he is still here? I have looked at the puppies, they all came over to greet me and put their paws against the glass, wagging their little tails. Wouldn't you prefer a much friendlier animal? With a puppy you know you will be getting eternal devotion, with this one..."

"*Señor*[1] Cantora, people haven´t chosen him because of his colour. There are some superstitions about black cats, but there is absolutely nothing wrong with him. He is in excellent health."

"It´s amazing how ignorant people are, good and bad things happen whether you come across a black cat or not. He looks just right for a belated gift. I see he doesn´t have a name, Balou seems just right for him." I declare with a smile.

I look at Javier as I say this, he sighs and makes a comment to the shopkeeper about women always getting their way. The shopkeeper happily gets everything ready, managing to sell us all we need for the cat´s future care; he also proceeds to sell some things that are most unnecessary.

---

[1] Mister in Spanish.

THREE

BALOU

From the first moment that I set my open eye on him, I disliked him intensely. I proceeded to close it right back and not give that man any reason to want to take me, especially as I had heard I was going to be taken to the shelter. It had to be better than going anywhere with "Cold Eyes". Just as I had decided to go back to sleep, I felt another presence, so being of a curious nature, I gave one more chance to whoever had decided to peer in at me. When I opened my eyes, I fixed them on the newcomer. There was something about the way she looked that was really captivating and for the first time I didn't feel like going back to sleep, which was my favourite pastime. She must have felt the same way because I heard her say she wanted me, I perked up after hearing those words, no one had wanted me before. Could this be finally happening? Was I about to get my freedom?

"Cold Eyes" didn't seem to like the idea and was trying to get her to pick something else but she looked at me and said I was what she wanted. The man who had fed me and cleaned my box all this time took me out of it and handed me over to her. She held me and stroked me, I didn't mind the latter but I wished she would just put me down, I don't like being so far from the floor. She is new at this, but we are going to have to change that habit quickly. The man who had wanted to take me to the shelter gave them a lot of things he said I would need and that I liked. I wondered why if he felt I liked them so much; in all the time we had spent together he had never given them to me before. I felt a sense of freedom even though they put me in another box to take me out of the shop and go to my new home.

I was taken to my new home; in my new carrier, the journey was far more comfortable than my first car ride. My new carrier would with time symbolise an impending vet visit, so I came to hate it after a while. I was able to see quite a bit through the sides of carrier, so, when we arrived at what was to be my new home... I was shocked to see just how massive it was. Compared to the three bedroom apartment that I was born in, which I had actually thought was huge after spending those weeks in my glass container in the shop, this looked like a palace.

Of course, not to break old habits, I had cried all the way home. But as we arrived, there was no sound coming out of my open mouth. I was experiencing so many emotions at the same time; the joy of leaving the shop, the fear of my new life and the fact that I had a very distinct and clear feeling that there was something "not quite right" about the man who had driven us home in disapproving silence.

At first, I was put in a room with only my litter, water and food for company. I spent some time hiding in a cupboard, then when no one was with me I explored the rest of the room. Rosario came to sit with me very regularly; she would put out her hand so I could smell her whilst she would talk to me. Little by little, I got to know her and after a little while I would peek out from under the bed each time I heard the door open, I wanted to know who was coming in and then I could decide if I wanted to be seen or not. In all fairness, Javier, alias "Cold Eyes", tried to show some interest in me but I didn´t like him, I decided to keep well out of his way and not encourage any form of familiarity.

A short while later, I was let out of the room, I couldn´t believe my eyes. There were so many other rooms, so many large corridors I could run across and so many curtains to climb. I noticed people didn´t like me climbing curtains though, I was constantly being pulled down from them, but I kept trying to reach the top...when no one was looking, I´d race to the top and wait for them to get me down, it took me some time to perfect the return route. I spent so many hours just running around because there was so much to see and investigate, so many hiding places and sleeping spots, so many new things to smell.

The one place I loved being, was, in the kitchen. They had a woman who cooked for them; she would put me on a stool next to the worktop so I could see what she was doing. It was a warm and cozy room. Cook was my second favourite person in the house, she would pet me and say I was the cat she loved most in the whole world, I did wonder how many cats she actually knew. There was a door that led to outside, this was usually shut, but she let me out with her when she was going to throw away rubbish or pick vegetables from the large garden behind the kitchen. Rosario said I was too young to go out, but cook used to sneak me out with her. I loved lying down on the grass and sleeping while the sun just did it's work and warmed me up, there were so many things to chase in the big garden; leaves, butterflies, birds... You name it; if it moved, it was worth pursuing. So, it was no surprise that I was always looking for an opportunity to escape outside.

For the first three weeks I lived in the house, I didn't see too much of Rosario and since I had decided she was my favourite person in the world, this wasn't a satisfactory arrangement for me at all. She would wake up late, it was a good thing that she wasn't in charge of the most important meal of the day for me, which was breakfast. She would always look for me to pick me up for a cuddle. I still didn't like being picked up and had hoped she would see by the expression on my face what an unpleasant moment it was for me. I would follow her from room to room because I liked being near her, keeping a safe distance at all times and to avoid giving her the opportunity to pick me up. However, it was something she did whenever she saw me. I soon taught her that carrying me like a baby was not right, I needed to see the floor and things around me, I hated staring at the ceiling belly up. I did enjoy riding on her shoulder though, when she picked me up, I'd find a way to get on there and we would go round the house in this manner, a much better arrangement for me.

Javier on the other hand was different story; I stayed away from him, inevitably though, we sometimes did have to pass each other, at which times, I walked ahead as if he didn't exist. Whenever he tried to pick me up, I made sure he put me down quickly by decorating his arms with my claws. This did the trick every single time. When he complained to Rosario, she would question what he said as I had never scratched her, she told him that he must be doing something wrong or somehow hurting me.

I resorted to getting her out of bed earlier; I would go to her room in the mornings and watch her, she would just be staring at the ceiling or the wall, this could not be normal, someone spending so much time in bed, not actually sleeping, just looking at a fixed spot? There was something seriously wrong with this woman... I wasn't able to climb on to the bed as yet, I was still too small, so I'd cry out to be picked up. Once on the bed I would make such a fuss, running under the duvet and hunting her feet that she would laugh and get up, then our day would begin and I'd just follow her around; that is except for when she disappeared for a few hours.

FOUR

ROSARIO

Having Balou in my life these past few weeks has really made a great difference for me. I really don´t know what prompted me to conquer my apathy and actually make an effort to want him on the day I saw him in that glass cage, but now, I´m really glad I did. I suffer from depression and most days I don't have the strength to get out of bed, let alone do anything else. Somehow, this tiny, round creature has found a way to make me want to do that, he makes it impossible for me to spend endless hours just looking at nothing as he demands my constant attention; he does not like being ignored at all. I haven´t had cats before and I certainly had never seen one like him; I did my research on his breed and I can´t wait for him to get to his full adult size, the photographs that I saw online were impressive, the big round head and body, those yellow eyes that give them an owlish look. Everyone in the household has taken to him except Javier, for some reason he doesn´t like the cat but it seems to be mutual as Balou avoids crossing paths with him, in his particular scale of dislike, he seems to have put him on the same level as his carrier, which he hates as it is a reminder of unpleasant vet visits.

No one knows that I have lost the will to keep living; everything is all the same to me now and it's only Balou with his antics that can bring a smile to my face lately. Who could imagine what my life has turned into? Endless days of not being able to feel anything but despair and desolation, just waiting for the hours to pass by and for another long day to be over and another one to begin. No one can know what goes on behind the mask I have carefully fashioned that helps to cover my real emotions. Nobody has noticed that my smiles no longer light up my eyes; but, why would they? I have everything anybody could want or even dream of having. What possible excuse could I have for not being happy?

I am Rosario Dominguez Gonzalez, heiress to one of the largest and oldest fortunes in Spain and my family is considered one of the most elite in both the economic and social circles as well as one of the richest and most influential in Europe. Apart from my two university degrees, I also completed my master's and I speak four different languages. I am married to Javier Cantora Albacea who also comes from a very privileged family, his father is a renowned architect who runs a multinational company and is responsible for a number of well known and emblematic buildings around the globe. My husband is an extremely attractive man, tall, fit, with abundant light brown hair that normally falls on his forehead and green eyes, the kind that you can get lost in. I, on the other hand have the racial beauty of the women from the south of Spain, I have long, straight and very black hair and my eyes are almost the same colour. From what I have heard people say about me, I am considered one of the most elegant and beautiful women in the country. But what both my professional and my personal resumés doesn't say is that I have also become my husband's punch bag.

My family is from Sevilla, we own vineyards and orchards. We produce and export wine, olive oil and fruit. The exceptional quality of our products makes them sought after in both the local and international market and they can be found in most gourmet shops practically all over the world. Our product brand is ranked year after year among the best five in the world; we never, ever step down from that. We are what is considered "old money", apart from what we cultivate, our family owns a lot of land and property. My paternal great-grandfather started from scratch with a small vineyard, he had a passion for good wine and it was said that he felt he could do better than what was served at his table, this he did, what started as a hobby was something soon demanded among the people of his class, before long, word spread around and there was more demand than supply. When his sons were of age, Saul, my grandfather and his brother Pablo decided they didn´t want to just be landlords, they decided to continue with the work their father started and the empire was expanded by adding olive plantations and fruit orchards. By the time my father and his three brothers went into the family business, the brand was known everywhere. We are where we are today because they have worked very hard for everything we now have, standards have never been lowered. When my grandfather died fifteen years ago, my father, being the first-born, took the leadership role, although he has always worked hand in hand with his siblings and five of my older cousins. My father is an agricultural engineer, he is very much hands-on and enjoys being "in the field", so to speak, experimenting and researching new varieties of vine and fruits. Our ranch is full of trees that he has done grafts to or experimented on, I have so many memories of going with him to inspect the progress of the projects he was working on and listening to him explaining what he had done and hoped to achieve in each case, so it came as no surprise that my first degree was in Agricultural and Biological Engineering as I wanted to continue developing new strains with all the desired

--

characteristics that would set them aside from what was presently available in the market.

If my father came from a very privileged family, my mother on the other hand came from an extremely humble one. The kind where herself and her younger sister hardly ever had new clothes, they were always wearing the handouts of friends and relatives and everything was reused until nothing more could be gotten out of it, be it food or other essential commodities. Because of this, even though we were surrounded by wealth, she stayed grounded and brought us up only with what she thought was necessary and nothing else. I still remember my father constantly giving orders for people to be employed to help out in the kitchen and my mother not letting them enter into what was her territory. At social events, she looked as if she had never washed a plate in her life, but anyone who was a regular visitor to our house, knew that if they wanted to find Carmen, all they had to do was to follow the aroma to the kitchen. Another example comes to mind, when I got my driving license and my father asked what car I wanted, I answered a Ferrari, my mother raised an eyebrow and the next day, to my great chagrin and with an apologetic smile from my father I was handed the keys to a second-hand Ford Mondeo. I could go on and on about the life lessons I got from her, but what I had complained about all my life, helped me a lot when at the age of twenty one. I became a very rich young lady, it had taught me not to squander it all away. I have to add, that I take after my father, when it comes to spending, as my mother often tells us, it looks as if we have a hole in the palm of our hands and the money just falls through it. My dresser gives a testimony to that, but if it were not for my mother, I would not know how to apply the brakes on a lot of things.

I am the eldest of three children; I have a younger sister, Soledad and a brother, Miguel, he was named after my father as it is the custom in many families in Spain. We all picked career paths that would help us become part of the lifelong work of the family especially as we would inherit it together with the rest of our cousins one day and our aim is to keep up the high quality standards that those before us worked so hard to set. I also studied Marketing and Business administration at university, once I finished this; I went to USA to do my master's programme. That is where I met Javier, he was also doing the same thing. A mutual friend introduced us and almost immediately Javier showed an interest in me. I wasn't very keen as I had ended a relationship a few months earlier, all I wanted to do was to return home and start working, so at first it was just a friendship and I had no intention of it becoming anything more.

Both our families have been in the society pages of the media for as long as I can remember. Every special occasion was photographed for all the celebrity magazines. We were both used to being in the limelight and being the centre of attention. Each time I dated someone, the press would get wind of it and we would be pursued until proof was acquired, they investigated my suitors and would talk about them endlessly on various television programmes, this was sometimes useful as I'd find out secrets that had been carefully guarded and kept from me. Javier had also grown up in a similar situation, I knew about his existence because he was ever present in the gossip pages with one new girlfriend or another. So when we met, I really did not take him seriously as he had a playboy reputation. I had no intention of becoming one more of his discarded girlfriends; instead I concentrated on what I had gone to do in USA, study. I had so many ideas to improve our brands and explore new markets that I didn't really put my heart into the new friendship. My indifference must have made him want me even more and when we returned to Spain he kept coming to Sevilla to see me. I suppose we had reporters and paparazzi assigned to us because before I knew it, we had been branded a couple and were making the cover of all the important magazines.

Our wedding was said to have been the most viewed on national television, after that of the Crown Prince. People came from many countries to attend the wedding, there wasn't a single hotel with vacancies in Sevilla, all had been booked months ahead, our families didn't spare any expense to make our day extremely special. I look back and remember how happy and innocent I was then, before all that was to come. I can't bear to look at the wedding photographs because all they provoke in me is the desire to turn back the hands of the clock, but that is impossible.

Javier was working with his father in Madrid, so I moved there after we got married. My family has a Foundation in Sevilla and it was decided that a branch would be opened in Madrid and that I would run it. This was not the sector I had spent such a long time preparing myself to work in but it meant being near Javier and as I enjoy a challenge, the branch in Madrid of *Fundación Esperanza* [2] was launched. Now, five years later, we have successfully implemented various charity projects in South America and Africa, but there is a lot of work still to be done. My staff and I work endless hours to make sure everything runs smoothly.

Our wedding gift from my parents-in-law was the mansion we live in. Javier's father, Ernesto, designed it. He had designed most of the houses in the exclusive and well guarded estate. Each house is more impressive than the next; as neighbours, we have some of the most important and élite athletes, politicians and artists in the country. When we

---

[2] Hope Foundation

moved in, we spent a lot of time decorating and furnishing all four floors of the house.

    I can't pinpoint the exact moment when things started going wrong between us. We were so in love when we got married, but then I guess everyone thinks their love stories have been the most important in history or that no one has loved with the same intensity as they have. About a year after our wedding, I noticed a change in him; he would come home angry and would hardly speak to me. I tried to find out what was wrong but I would only get short answers or grunts. One moment he was like that and then suddenly it would seem as if a dark cloud had been lifted from him and he would be happy, charming and carefree again. I assumed he was stressed, he had a number of projects he was juggling at the same time, that had to be difficult as he had to meet deadlines, this didn't always depend on how well he did his job but on other external factors. I tried to be supportive and understand what he was working on at the time. I thought things would get better, but I have learnt that if things can get worse, then they will. It seemed he would pick arguments for the smallest things and blow them out of proportion, he would shout at me and over time he became abusive. At first I would try to placate him but like most women from the south, I too have a fierce character and temper. I felt he was pouring out his frustrations on me and I really didn't deserve that, after all that's what he went to the gym for, to let off steam. Nobody had ever spoken to me or treated me in such a way before; I had been brought up to be respectful but not to accept any form of abuse from anyone.

I still remember the first time he hit me, I had been in a meeting with some of our patrons in Madrid, had barely got home on time to oversee the preparations for a dinner we were giving that evening. We have very competent staff at home and I had gone over every detail with them that morning, but our chauffeur, Juan had got the wrong bottles of wine. I know my wines as I grew up with them and know what to combine with each meal. A good wine will always bring out the taste of whatever you serve; it can make or break a social event. It was an honest mistake and although I would have preferred it not to have happened, especially taking into consideration my family's reputation, it did; still we all had a pleasant evening. However, Javier didn't share my opinion, he was charming while our guests were around but as soon as they left, he called in Juan and was quite abusive to him. I intervened because I felt that he was humiliating him unnecessarily and that's when he turned on me. I suppose we had both drunk a little too much and that had helped to heighten tempers and emotions. In a short while we were both screaming at each other, Juan, the poor man, was just standing there watching us, he was asked in a not very nice way to leave. By then, Javier had made it clear that it was all my fault, if I had been home then the mistake would not have happened. I was shocked when I heard him say that, he knew that I worked and that the meeting I had had that day was very important, I told him that had he gotten home before me, he could have checked too. That was when he hit me, in that moment a silence reigned in the room and we both looked at each other, I couldn't believe what had just happened, how could it have reached that point? Most important, how had he dared to raise his hand at me?

I was lost for words, I remember turning around and stumbling out of the room. That night, I locked myself in one of the spare rooms while he spent most of the night pounding at the door asking me to please let him in so we could talk. The next day he was full of apologies, he couldn´t explain what had gotten into him, he kept saying how much he regretted his actions, he couldn´t understand what had come over him and he couldn´t even remember the exact moment that he had hit me. What was I to do then? I wanted desperately to believe that it had indeed been the alcohol, that it was something that would never have happened under normal circumstances and above all, I loved him. So of course I forgave him, it was an isolated incident, never to occur again.

But it has occurred, over and over again. We have been married for five years and now the masks have been dropped. There is no more pretending, I have gained the status of being in a physically and emotionally abusive relationship. We don't need the wrong wine on the table to cause an argument, now he just looks for excuses to fight. I am a shadow of my former self and I don't bother replying to his attempts to quarrel but I still get beaten, whenever things go wrong, I pay for them. He has stopped apologising, he seems to feel that it is normal and that I have to live with it, I'm scared because I'm beginning to think that it is part of life and that somehow I deserve it.

I haven't told a soul about it. My father would kill him; if he knew what had gone on. He wouldn't wait for any court to condemn him, he is a man who fights for and protects his family with everything he has. I would never place him in a position in which he would be held accountable for taking another man's life, even if that life was Javier's.

My mother, however, is very religious and I'm afraid that she would frown on my leaving him; she would tell me I had to accept such a treatment from my husband as apart from being a God fearing woman, she is also quite traditional in some aspects. We are a close knit family and her approval means the world to me. I have a lot of friends, I consider that my very close ones are those I went to school with and thankfully they are in Sevilla so I have avoided meeting them although they have pushed for an all girls reunion, threatening to come to Madrid and see me. When I have gone home for Christmas we have met up for dinner or lunch but somehow I can´t bring myself to open my mouth and say the words that are constantly on my mind because at the end of the day, I have a lot of pride and I couldn't stand being the recipient of the looks of pity that are normally given out to women and children who are unfortunate enough to find themselves being part of domestic violence. So I smile and say that everything is going well, I tell them that I want to hear all about them as I already know what is going on in my life. The "friends" I have made in Madrid I can keep more at arm's length as either I met them through Javier and socialized with them through him or I have done so through the Foundation and charity events, either way, they are the ones I owe an explanation to the least. Also, I have come to realise that people don't wash their dirty linen in public, everybody is fine and their marriage is perfect, they will swear to this, even if they announce a divorce two weeks later citing irreconcilable differences.

When Javier is happy, everyone else has to be too. He gets all excited and makes grand gestures towards me. People used to say that when I smiled, my whole face would light up. I wonder if he has noticed that I no longer smile. Now they say I use make up more than I did before, I have got used to having to expertly hide the bruises so no one can notice them.

--

We have been married for five years and don't have children. At first I felt that if I had them, I wouldn't be so alone but now I'm extremely glad that they didn't come. How could I allow someone I love so much to see the way I'm being treated or to have to live in fear like me? Doctors and specialists have told me that there is absolutely nothing wrong with me but I know that my constant state of anxiety and tension is responsible. When we meet up to celebrate Christmas or family birthdays, everyone asks us what we are waiting for, they think we are still in the honeymoon phase of our relationship, especially as Javier always has his arm around me. It's ironic that I once found that gesture romantic, now it just feels like I'm a prisoner serving a lifelong sentence with no hope for parole.

I have long since stopped trying to find an explanation for his behaviour; he is simply a bad person who enjoys watching me suffer. I have even searched for drugs around the house as this would be an explanation for his mood swings and his apparent memory loss, if he has a habit, then he hides it very well as I have not been able to find proof of it.

The staff look at me with pity; I read it on their faces. Our house is big but is impossible not to at least suspect what is going on, especially as we spend more and more time sleeping in separate bedrooms and we hardly talk, except when necessary or in public to keep up appearances.

They are extremely kind to me; it is their way of trying to make up for a part of my life they don't have the power to change.

Yet the press have tagged us as one of the happiest and most glamorous couples on the social scene. I really think that actresses that have won Oscars have not played half as good a role as I have, I have beat them hands down as I have been able to convince everyone, that my life is perfect, even those closest and dearest to me.

So you see, I really don't have a reason for getting out of bed, I just want this life to be over as soon as possible and for the days to pass quickly. Every day is just the same, a painful reminder of my present reality, of the dreams that will never come to pass and of all that could have been.

FIVE

BALOU

I have been here for four months now. In this time I have worked very hard to train my humans, this has not been an easy task but it's something we cats make sure we do to avoid misunderstandings. They need a lot of patience on my part before they can get to the point that allows me to live in the comfort and style that I deserve. It is important they handle me with utmost care, I have made sure everyone knows my feeding schedules and they also know that they have to be on time, I don't accept delays of any kind in this department. They have also been taught that I have allocated time for cuddles, but I also love my privacy and if anyone takes time to read my body language, bloodshed in any form can be avoided. As you can see, they are very simple guidelines and anyone with even a minimum amount of intelligence should be able to follow them.

My biggest hurdle has been Rosario; sometimes she sleeps in a room with Javier, on those nights I am not allowed in. There are a lot of days that she sleeps by herself, in a smaller room than the one they share and at these times I am permitted to be with her. I sense a great sadness in her and have noticed that she spends a lot of time crying. I sit by her side and watch her, she holds me, sometimes too tight so I try to remember to sit a little out of reach, but still near enough to comfort her with my presence. She spends a lot of hours in that room, even when it is day time. It is such a waste, we could be outside running, chasing birds and butterflies or simply soaking up the sun. So I've taken it upon myself to help her see this because I can get people to do what I want. I have learnt that they find it difficult to deny me things, all the staff in the house at one time or another during the day look for me because they feel the need to give me a pat or a cuddle. Aside from Rosario and Javier, there are four other people that I see every day.

Juan is the driver or chauffeur as he likes to call himself. He is a tall, slender man with curly black hair and sideburns to match. He also has dimples that I love watching each time he smiles. He spends most of his time outdoors in the front garden cleaning the three cars, he will sit in them reading or sometimes even sleeping. He also runs errands when either one of his employers need something. I have seen both Javier and Rosario drive their own cars but sometimes he takes them to places. He is a pleasant young man who comes in to the kitchen every day, this is my favourite spot in the house; he'll have his breakfast or a cup of coffee. When I hear his voice, I normally rush to say hello and rub myself against his legs, it's a routine we have. He always picks me up, throws me in the air and then places me on his shoulder. I can´t say I care much for the throwing me in the air part but I love being on his shoulders; we then go out into the garden and I can watch everything from a totally different perspective, from this position it's easier to watch the birds perched on the tree branches, I can spend time calculating the distance between me and them, I think Juan sees my intention as he quickly moves away from the area of interest. Whenever he puts me down, I run to try and climb one tree or the other and for some strange reason I can´t get back down, I meow loudly to get his attention when it´s time for me to be rescued. I also love being inside the cars while he cleans them, there is so much to smell and investigate and sometimes I pounce on the cloth that Juan is using to shine a car. He doesn´t let me into Javier´s car as he has been given instructions not to allow me to. I have had a number of opportunities to go in and leave him a little "present" but I really don´t want to get my friend into trouble as I know he will get all the blame and I have other ways of punishing Javier anyway.

Adela is the cook, she is a stout red headed woman who spends all her time in the kitchen and she seems to really enjoy what she does. She has also been put in charge of my breakfast, as lately Rosario does not come out of her room, her meals are taken to her on a tray which sometimes comes back exactly how it left. The good thing is that Javier leaves early for work, she has to serve him his breakfast at seven o clock in the morning, this is a most suitable and convenient time for me to have mine, so I normally walk past him sitting in the big dining room on my way to the kitchen, he always gets a look from me that speaks volumes. If he has not yet read between the lines then he is even more stupid than I imagined, which believe me, would be difficult. I know he is the cause of Rosario´s unhappiness and one way or the other; I will put a stop to it! Adela is my second favourite person in the house, although sometimes it´s a tie with Juan. She is always laughing and this causes her whole body to shake. She has set up a high stool for me near the kitchen counter so I can watch her while she works, this is something she knows I love doing and I spend a lot of time by her side. Every once in a while she envelops me in her big strong arms to give me a hug, she tells me she can´t resist me and chuckles when she sees the look of sheer indignation on my face, but I can´t help it, I keep going back for more because I am a vain creature and not ashamed to admit it, I just love being told how handsome I am.

Marylin and Marcos are the other two people that come to my abode on a daily basis. They are a married Filipino couple that take care of the cleaning, I am a bit wary of them as once I heard Adela ask them if they ate cat meat in their country as she watched a documentary about unusual recipes. Marylin said she had never done it but she knew of people who had, apparently they prefer other delicacies, but if it is true that I´m so well formed as I´m being constantly told, then I don´t want to be a temptation to anyone! They might just be the type of people who just say what others want them to say and might be looking for the chance to whisk me away and I certainly do not want to end my days in somebody´s cooking pot. So I keep a safe distance even though they give me a friendly pat on my head each time they see me.

When Rosario sleeps in the big room with Javier and I´m not let in, I wander around the house and choose the spot where I want to spend the night or a part of it, one of the things I enjoy doing most is running up and down the very long corridors and the stairs, something Javier complains about, although I don´t know how it could disturb him when he closes the door in my face at night. Yes dear reader, you did not misunderstand the words you are so engrossed in, I follow Rosario everywhere she goes when she is up and when it's time to sleep and she goes to the bedroom, I also try to walk in with her, but he is ever ready to shut me out. At that precise moment, we both look at each other and there is a wicked smile on his face. So in return, I spend a lot of time running up and down the house because I feel like doing it, but also because I know he hates it. Whilst I do it I imagine him covering his ears with a pillow. I have heard him complaining about it on several occasions, Rosario defends me saying "he's just a kitten and it's what they do; play and amuse themselves with everything..." That man is just plain ignorant, but no matter, I have a lot of time to educate and train him.

SIX

ROSARIO

Javier has been in a good mood for the past three weeks, which means that he hasn't hit me in all that time, he has been especially attentive, sending me flowers and forcing me to go out to dinner, the theatre, for drinks, to parties... One would think that I would be able to relax more but it's quite the opposite, it's just like a green snake under the grass, you never see it coming until it's too late. That is how I feel, I'm on edge, waiting to be bitten by the snake, wondering what word, look or action of mine will trigger a beating, but he seems to be in extremely high spirits. I don't dare to ask the reason or contradict him, I just go where he wants and I keep quiet. This means I meet a lot of people who know us; they come over to speak to us all the time. In these past five years I have perfected the lie of pretending everything is perfect and fine, a few photographs make the gossip pages and I actually laughed out loud when I read the caption to one of them "Javier and Rosario as in love as the first day they met". I guess people need to believe in fairy tales and they need to see that others are happy. I wish I could scream out my truth to the world and expose him for the lying, manipulative, evil, wife beater he is. I think about it all the time, I imagine being in a gathering of extremely important people and just blurting it all out while he stands there helpless, unable to stop me, then everyone walks out on him with a look of disgust on their faces ostracizing him from their lives forever.

I am full of mixed and contradictory emotions, anger at him that he dares treat me in such a way, disbelief at myself that I have let it go on for such a long time, shame that anyone should find out, fear for what it may do to the people I love if this is known, pity for myself because a part of me still likes it when he treats me like he used to before all this began and uncertainty at when this situation will explode again.

After an absence of three and a half months, I finally go to the office again. During all that time that I hid myself from the world; my staff and I communicated through emails and phone calls, all the documents I had to sign were delivered to my home and I sent them back once I had read them via Juan. But now I feel it is necessary for me to go back into the real world, decisions have to be made and I need to be there, so I have decided to go in this morning and surprise them. When I walk into the reception area, Marisa who is at the front desk looks up in surprise, it dawns on me then just how long I have been gone and that in the staff's eyes I have probably become one of those absent bosses who just collects a pay cheque without really knowing how to run the company or what is really going on, leaving all the work to others but taking all the credit for everything. I hope this is not the case and that I have proven just how competent I am or rather have been in the past. She gets up to greet me and we exchange two kisses, as is the custom, I then ask her to gather everyone in the board room in half an hour and make my way to my office at the end of the corridor. Pilar my personal assistant is on the phone and she smiles at me as she waves her hand energetically in greeting, I go into my office, sit behind my desk and switch on my computer. I have been checking my emails from home, so I'm not so far behind but I have a huge pile of letters to go through. Just as I'm about to open one, Pilar comes in and I repeat the same process I did with Marisa.

"You are back! I was wondering when you would pass by. I hope everything is fine, I know you sometimes take time off and work from home but I don´t think it has ever been this long."

"Everything is fine; I just have a lot on my plate. How have you been?"

"I´m fine but my mother isn´t."

"What is wrong?"

"She had a stroke two days ago and is in intensive care."

"Why did you come to work? You should be with your mother and the rest of your family. I´m sure we can manage perfectly without you for a few days. You are not helping her here and I´m sure you can´t even concentrate in your work. Please go and stay with her, I had no idea, you should have told me."

"I need the distraction; we are only allowed to visit her for half an hour in the morning and another half an hour in the evening and everyone wants to go in. My two brothers, my sister, my father, my uncles and aunts..."

"What do the doctors say?"

"That she is in a critical condition, you know how they are, they never let on anything until the patient is out of the woods. We are all just praying so much for her to make it. But enough about me, how have you been? Aside from the few calls and many emails we have exchanged, I don´t know what you have been up to. You look as if you have lost weight, have you been ill?"

"No, really I´m fine, it must be the stress of the day to day running of things, you know how it is with us women, we add and lose weight at an alarming speed."

"Speak for yourself, I don´t seem to shed any, I just add and add, I´m on a new diet now but all the fat seems to concentrate in the same place."

I laugh as Pilar looks down sorrowfully at her middle region. She is on the plump side, has a really pretty face and is a smallish woman. She is the personification "of the girl next door", the kind of girl a nice boy would always go back to look for when he wanted to settle down, but Pilar has not been lucky with boys. She always set her hopes high when starting a new relationship but they are usually dashed soon after. I know that it is because she is just too nice a person and doesn´t understand that not everyone approaches her with the best of intentions.

It feels good to be back to work and out of that tension filled house, where all we do is pretend that everything is perfect. I need this, to be able to laugh and submerge myself in work, especially as we are helping so many people. A knock on the door brings me out of my thoughts and Marisa comes in to tell us that everyone is in the Board room waiting for us. Pilar follows me with her pad to take notes, assuming her professional role by my side.

When we get there, everyone gets up to say hello before we all sit down. There are ten of us working for the Foundation although Sergio and Pablo are in Guatemala supervising the food bank we opened a month ago. Both of them travel to our projects regularly to make sure everything is working in accordance with the reports we are getting from the local correspondents. We are very serious about the work we do and do not want to put our trust in other people to avoid situations that can spoil the good name of our company and family. So many cases are brought to light of NGO´S and similar organisations that are not being as honest as they should; we will not be one of the many that are brought down by one greedy middleman or intermediary; we prefer to personally supervise everything that is done in the name of *Fundación Esperanza*.

Marisa remains at the front desk, Pilar will brief her later of what was discussed so she can tell our patrons and donors when they call to ask for updates. After enquiring about the other five workers present, I ask them to give me a summary of the projects that have been assigned to them.

I oversee everything but find that it is easier if each person has an area of expertise, that way they devote all their time to making sure it works perfectly. We run a local food bank that opens two Saturdays a month. Since the economic crisis took hold, a lot of people have lost their jobs and are finding it very difficult to make ends meet, some have had to give up their homes as they have been unable to pay the monthly mortgage, we decided that helping out with food would take a small part of their worries away from them. We have a rented office and shop in the city centre which we use as a storage facility; it is also open twice a week to receive applications from families that need help. We are also working with our local parish; they have sent us a great number of families who have become constant visitors to the facilities. Ana is in charge of this, she is a forty-year old widow who has no children of her own, she says that she is really happy to be able to devote her time to this project as when her husband died, she felt like she had lost her direction in life, she needed something to get her out of the state of desperation she found herself in. She is a very hard worker and tells me that she needs help as she can't cope with everything, especially those two Saturdays in the month as a lot of people come in. I tell her that I will look into things and see if we can hire someone part-time. Daniel, Oscar and Sarah all have projects in Africa and South America, both education and health related, we have a mobile clinic in Angola, which goes from village to village, this is my father's pet project as he once visited the country and decided this was a very good way to help and reach as many people as possible, Sarah is in charge of this. Daniel and Oscar are working to get school material to under-privileged schools in South America. Everyone explains what they have been up to, though I have followed things closely. Even when I have not felt like doing anything, I dragged myself out of bed to read emails or make calls, this job is the only good thing I have and I can't give Javier the satisfaction of watching it crumble because he has made me incapable of doing my work, something tells me he would be really happy if this happened. I look at Valentina as she is the last to speak, I'm not very keen on her project as it is too close to home. She runs the training scheme we have started for victims of domestic violence, it's funny how I started it after a horrible fight with Javier which at the time had some painful consequences for me. I realised that I had an education and a family to turn to but a lot of women don't have that choice, they have to put up with extremely horrible situations. I don't like knowing what is going on, I don't want to put a face to the victims or hear any stories that I can relate to. I just want to help them, but from a distance.

"We have been able to get work promises from two supermarkets and a floor tile manufacturing company. They will start with temporary contracts and if it goes well, they might offer more stability to the women."

--

"That is very good news. Well done."

"Also the National Association for domestic violence is having a gala dinner to give out awards to people who have worked really hard this year in trying to help women and children that have suffered domestic abuse. You are one of the award winners, I sent you an email about it, I don´t know if you saw it as I didn´t get any reply but I need to confirm your attendance as soon as possible."

I look up sharply when she says this, I don´t want to go. Of course I saw the email but I didn´t reply hoping it would just go away. I had completely forgotten about it, if not I would have stayed away one more week until after the event and just said I had not received the email, I know Valentina called the house several times but I hadn´t returned the calls. The last thing I want is to go and face women that have found the courage to walk away from a situation that I have been unable to. I would feel like a hypocrite. I must have been silent for more than I thought because when I looked up everyone was staring at me; I found I couldn't say anything but "of course, I would be honoured to accept the award."

SEVEN

BALOU

Every day, I still find new places to explore, it's such a big house, you would think I would have seen it all after five months but just when I think I have, I discover a new cupboard to investigate or a corner of a room I haven't visited before. So, in the hours of the day that I'm not paying respect to the Spanish tradition of the siesta, I am really busy exploring.

I'm quite happy with Rosario, she has gradually been coming out of her shell. At first, it was to leave the house with that horrid Javier, I didn't get the impression that she was particularly pleased at the prospect of being alone in his company, but then she started going out without him, she would leave in the morning and come back in the evening tired but happy. She always ran to look for me and pick me up, sometimes before it was the official time for me to wake up. Now this is something that I don't tolerate in anyone else but I grudgingly do with her. Seeing her smile once again is worth it, I must admit though that sometimes I do look for places to sleep that are very difficult for her to gain access to, somewhere I can relax without being disturbed but somehow she always ends up finding me. She throws me in the air and puts me on her shoulder, while she complains about how big and heavy I am becoming. This is one of my favourite moments of the day as it gives me a totally different perspective on the world, so I purr away happily while I go with her to see and do things around the house. She always feeds me in the evening and I know just where my food is kept, I know the routine, so I quickly jump to the kitchen counter next to the cupboard where the food tins are kept and I meow away to hurry her up. She watches me while I eat, she has a smile on her face and she tells me how lucky she is to have me and that I have her. I don't want to spoil that feeling for her but Juan and Cook, also think exactly the same thing, oh well, there is no need to make them think any different is there? There is a lot of me to go round. After dinner I lead her to get my brush so she can groom me, then we play my favourite game of hide and seek, in which I hide behind doors and as she doesn't know where I am, I jump at her or I run away and she chases me trying to catch me. All this we do when that horrible man is not around, he seems not to like the fact that Rosario is besotted with me; she knows this, so we play it cool when he is home. I shadow her and sit near her all the time because I sense her tension, I haven't been able to understand why, but "Cold Eyes" just keeps emitting negative vibes, even when he is smiling or laughing, it is there, beneath the surface. I have a lot of power in my limbs and my jaws and though I am of stocky build, my appearance is quite deceptive, I move much faster than is expected of me. We hold staring competitions and I always win, we look at each other in a challenging way, the silly man thinks I will look away first but I have all the time in the world, I have the natural instinct to hunt things that move and I can spend a long time watching and waiting for the perfect moment.

Rosario receives a phone call that makes her very happy, she tells me as she picks me up that her parents are coming and they are finally going to meet me. There is a lot of activity in the next two days as every nook and cranny is being cleaned and one of the spare rooms where I usually nap is prepared for them. Rosario spends time with Adela in the kitchen elaborating on endless lists of things her parents like to eat; I hardly see Marylin and Marcos with all the work they have to do. Everything is perfect although I do try to leave a few hairs here and there to make them feel more at home. How else will they tell people that they have been to a house with a cat?

    Finally, the car pulls up on the drive way, Juan was sent to collect them from the airport, he gets out of the car first and opens the back doors for them. Juan looks so smart and professional in his suit and tie, he smiles at me when he sees I have come out to see what the new arrivals look like. Rosario runs forward to hug and kiss the man and woman who get out of the car, while that hateful man stands back, next to me. I move away as the last thing I want is for him to draw any comfort from my presence, he is very uneasy, that I can tell.

    The man is huge, by his side the woman looks like the dot on the letter i, she is not as slim as Rosario but not as big as Adela either, they are both excited to see her. I can tell that they are genuinely fond of her by the way they hold her and look her over to see how she is; they look at her with real affection. I want to tell them that she is not that fine as "Cold Eyes" seems to be causing her a lot of unhappiness, but if there is one gift that the good Lord did not bless me with, it's speech. When they have finished greeting her, Javier walks over, shakes her father's hand and gives her mother one kiss on each cheek. They talk to him a little and then I decide it's time they met me, so I slowly and gracefully make my way towards them; they all suddenly stop and look at me.

"What a beauty, he looks like a mini version of a panther. Can I pick him up? Does he bite?"

"He doesn´t like being picked up much but I do it all the time, here let me pass him to you."

And with those words, I am unceremoniously and abruptly lifted from the ground, ending my majestic entrance, Rosario passes me to her mother who hugs me and kisses my head repeatedly while her husband is looking at me very closely.

"I think you are overfeeding him. He looks too fat and his head is very round, should it be so big?"

"No papa, that is how this breed is, they are more muscular and heavy built than the cats you are used to seeing. Notice how his legs are shorter, I have consulted with the vet and checked online and he is well within the weight range for his breed."

"If you say so, it doesn't look like he can run well. Is he a good mouser? All those good looks mean nothing if he can´t hunt and keep the house free of rodents."

"Ha ha, papa you are so funny, we don´t have mice in the house. A company comes in periodically to fumigate against all kinds of pests. Let's go in so you can freshen up, lunch is almost ready. We are having your favourite today in honour of your visit, *Paella*[3]."

We all go in; I am still crushed in her mother´s arms while her father is looking at me with a raised eyebrow; probably still wondering what I´m useful for.

---

[3] Typical Spanish dish made with rice and sea food, although some regions of Spain make different versions with vegetables, chicken and or rabbit.

EIGHT

ROSARIO

I´m so happy my parents are here. As soon as they learnt that I was going to be given an award, they told me that they would come and spend a few days with us and accompany us to the ceremony. We had a lovely lunch and while the men stay back with their coffees and liquor, my mother and I go to the other sitting room where we are served ours, so we can talk freely. As we live in different cities that are so far apart, coupled with the fact that my parents work a lot and that Javier does not like me going to visit them alone, I normally just see my parents for two weeks in the summer when we go to Sevilla and at Christmas when we all gather together for a family celebration. My mother has visited on only a few occasions in the five years I have been married and living in Madrid, she doesn't like to leave my father and my siblings alone; she has people that help her with the house work but she is the kind of woman who needs to be ever present to supervise everything. She also has a very active role in the branch of the Foundation we have in Sevilla. The fact that we are separated by such a distance has helped me a great deal with concealing my situation. I have had to work really hard to always present a cheerful countenance to my family, especially as very little gets past my mother. When I first arrived in Madrid, we would talk every day. I missed them terribly but when things started going downhill, I just couldn´t face pretending everything was perfect, especially with my mother. With the excuse that I had a lot of work and also needed time to settle in Madrid, I started spacing the calls further and further apart and when she complained I promised to send a daily message which made things much easier for me. Written words can hide a multitude of sins. Now that things seem to be going better with Javier, or at least his good mood is lasting longer than usual, their visit couldn´t have come at a better time. My thoughts are interrupted when she touches my arm gently as she has evidently been asking me something.

"You have lost weight. Why? You know you don´t need to. Have you been ill or something?"

"No, it just happened. I haven't done anything special, I guess it's the stress of work, the home..."

"Well you need to slow down then, it's not healthy to look so skinny. These days you modern girls want to look as if you have not eaten for three weeks and you think it is attractive. I can see all your collarbones and ribs. Well, let me tell you, it's not pleasant to look at."

I smile while my mother keeps on talking, she is so down-to-earth and has a no nonsense way of saying things, it took me back to my childhood when we would come home with an unreasonable request about something we wanted to do or get, just because our friends were doing it. She would give us replies that left no room for arguments because there were just no loopholes in her rules.

"I am fine; I will try to slow down so as not to be even less attractive than I am now so when you come to see me you can say, you have a daughter that makes heads turn."

"Ah, now you are laughing at me but I can tell you that I don't like what I see and it worries me. I am your mother and that gives me the right to tell you things that probably no one else can. Gain a few kilos; even your skin has lost its usual glow. This doesn't mean that you are not looking as pretty as ever but for me your health and happiness comes first. By the way, when are you going to make me a grandmother?"

I am not at all surprised by the question, especially as she does not beat around the bush when she wants to say something. My mother believes that time wasted is never recovered so she doesn't spend five minutes trying to get to a certain topic, she just asks away.

"I have no idea; the doctors have said that we are both healthy and that there is nothing wrong with us, so I guess it is just a matter of time."

"Maybe it's a matter of working too much and coming home too tired."

"It really isn't that."

"Fine, I know everyone is asking you the same thing and it must be quite uncomfortable for you. I just hope that if there is something wrong, you'd tell me. It is very difficult for a woman to bear that burden alone. I'm not just trying to be nosey, that is just a small part of it."

"I know, you can ask me what you want, I just don't have any answers for you. You can change that worried look, I have no secret illness that I'm going to reveal to you all on my death bed."

"How is Javier? He seemed a bit quiet at lunch, is everything fine?"

"He has a lot of work and deadlines to meet, sometimes it´s a lot of pressure. He works till very late and when he is home, he is usually on the phone getting things done. In this economic crisis, we all have to work even harder to convince the clients that the job can still be done and that they can trust us. Which means more hours of work and for the same money or even less, there is a lot of competition and if you don´t pull your weight someone else will get the project and the contract. Javier and Ernesto have a solid reputation but the crisis has also had an effect on them, people look for cheaper alternatives."

"I know, lots of companies are shutting down, it´s sad to see the state of things, your father says in a few years things will pick up and for once I wish time wouldn't move so slowly. But enough about serious things, we are so proud of you. We keep getting calls from our patrons telling us how well you and your team are handling the projects, they are especially happy about the fact that they get a monthly detailed newsletter explaining all the work that is being done. I know that was your idea, it really makes me happy to be able to give you credit. I am planning a fundraiser next month for the soup kitchen in Guatemala, I will show you all I´ve written down and the ideas I´ve come up with. We are also planning a cooking competition and an all day bake sale to raise funds for the families that we help in our parish in Sevilla. You can't imagine the number of people who are coming in to ask for help for even the most basic needs, good hard working families that have nowhere else to turn to."

She opens her big and tattered green agenda where she writes down everything. Every year she buys a new replacement set of pages, she has many new and better quality ones that we have all bought for her on various occasions, we are ashamed that she should bring out her shabby looking one in public, but she keeps using it. I do understand the sentimental value of it though, as her mother gave it to her many years ago and it holds a very special meaning as they were very close. We happily talk about all her plans, my mother normally holds three fundraisers a year, because of the importance and power of my family, she knows a lot of influential people will give their support. In all honesty, we really don't need outside help to fund our projects but once people started hearing about things that we were doing, we started getting requests to help out, some explained to us that they had looked for ways to help out but needed to find people they could trust, it feels good to know that they have put their confidence in our work. She also tells me all that is going on at home and how my siblings are doing, they both send me their congratulations, they would have come but are sitting for their exams in university, but they promise to visit me afterwards. She also fills me in with all the local news and gossip. I can't express in words how good their visit makes me feel, I normally don't invite people over because of my situation, I don't know what they might find, if one day Javier's rage makes him act out in public what he does in private or in case they see me and read between the lines. Although, so far I am the only privileged one that he has let see his true nature. I have wondered if he has some sort of mental disorder that he isn't aware of, if this is the case maybe he can get help? I don't understand how he can be so charming now when not so long ago, he would look at me with pure hatred. I have read a lot online trying to find something that can explain it all, that can make me feel like it's not my fault, that I don't have something in me that triggers such violent reactions in him. I've read countless stories of abused women and the more I read the more I'm convinced that I have to stop looking for reasons to explain his behavior, he is just a cruel and sadistic man.

I'm still not looking forward to attending the gala tomorrow night, I feel so weak when I am near those women and such a coward. If this had not happened to me, I would be the first to say that it is their fault for letting things go so far, that they need to think of their safety and walk away. Yet here I am, rooted to the same place with so many fears about what might happen. The only positive thing is that we are helping someone to find a life after what they have gone

--

through and a small part of me feels responsible for those women and children, I have to be part of the solution even if it's for someone else. Funny how it is so much easier to help and decide what others should do, but when it comes to oneself, it is a completely different story.

The next evening when we arrive at the gala we all pass through the photo-call, there is a lot of press; photographers and reporters each identified by the TV station they represent. A lot of celebrities have been invited; some who really help out and some who just use the opportunity to promote themselves and leave almost immediately their photographs have been taken. After posing for the press and answering a few questions we are shown to our table, there we greet the people who are to be seated with us, an ex-beauty-queen, her husband and a well-known businessman and his girlfriend.

We have lovely evening, even though I am tense, the food and the company are great and the presenters of the gala, who work on a very popular talk show, introduce and speak about the work that the various winners and organisations have done to help the victims of domestic abuse. We are called up one by one and given our prizes, a glass pyramid on an engraved metallic base. The eight award winners all give a little speech, I dedicated mine to the Foundation and my family in general, it feels really wrong to single out Javier and thank him, when it is because of people like him we have to hold ceremonies like this in the first place.

When I get back to my seat the people at our table all congratulate me and we collectively talk about the work the various NGO´S and the Government are doing to try to help people who find themselves in such extreme situations. Thankfully, there is much more awareness now; what was seen before as something that happened, but had to be kept behind closed doors, is now considered a crime. Our society has come a long way, even though there is still much more ground to cover. The ex-beauty-queen and I talk about how it´s a shame that jail sentences for such offenders are not longer and harsher. Whilst we talk, I notice that Javier is listening intently to our conversation. I saw him clap while I was speaking on stage; I wonder what was going through his mind at that moment and how he could have been so cynical to have come to the gala in the first place. If I had been in his shoes I´d have made any excuse I could think of not to have come. When he looks in the mirror what does he see? Because it seems to be something completely different to what I would expect him to see.

My thoughts are interrupted by the presenter announcing that the evening could not be complete without hearing from the people that are responsible for bringing us together for such a great cause. Four women come up to the stage and everyone stands up, the applause they receive is deafening. Then, there is silence while we all sit down, you could have heard a pin drop as the first woman approached the microphone. There is a gigantic screen behind her that during dinner has shown the different facilities available to women and children that are in need of help and have nowhere to go; the images are accompanied by the phone numbers that should be called to get help. Suddenly, the images are replaced by a photograph of a young couple smiling on their wedding day...

"My name is Julia Gómez Sánchez, the photograph behind me was taken eight years ago, the day I got married, the smile on my face was real, at that moment I was immensely happy and so in love with that man sitting next to me. Now that I have finally been able to escape what I can only imagine hell must be like, I can say out loud that I have never in my life felt so much fear or hatred for anyone. We got married very young, against my parent's wishes; they wanted me to finish school and get a degree; to be ready for the real world, but I was in love and I thought I knew everything. I thought that because they were older, they had forgotten what that felt like, so they found it difficult to put themselves in my shoes, but I stood my ground and they finally gave in after countless arguments, they did not want to lose me. At first everything was just as I had imagined, he worked in a fish shop and I got a job in a hairdressing saloon, we rented a small apartment, we didn´t have much but we were so happy. Then just six months after our second child was born, he lost his job and no matter how much he tried he didn´t seem to be able to get another one that would last for more than a week. He started drinking, he would disappear for hours and I wouldn't know where he had been or what he had done. We fought a lot, at first it was just angry words and we would make up soon after, but then he started hitting me and I saw in his eyes from the way he looked at me and our two children that he blamed us for his misfortunes, we were a dead weight to him. We kept out of his way as much as we could, I tried to stay away as long as possible from home with the children as I didn´t want them to be in such a toxic environment, hoping he´d be passed out when we got home from the park or from taking a walk; we walked aimlessly up and down different streets. I always tried to shut them in another room with the TV as loud as possible when their father decided that I was a good substitute for a punching bag. I thought things would change, we had two children; at some point he had to realise that they were worth fighting for. He broke my nose, several ribs and I lost the hearing completely in my left ear. Each time I went to the emergency ward, the doctors kept questioning me about who had done this to me because it was their duty to report it to the police, which they did, but they had to release me because my version of the events was always that I had fallen down or hit myself against a glass door that I had not seen, even though the bruises on my body told a completely different story. I still remember one doctor telling me with tears in his eyes that he didn´t want to go and have to identify me in the mortuary, but I strongly believed that things could be different; he just needed for his luck to change. I needed to believe that one day everything was going to be alright, the alternative was to accept that I had made a really horrible mistake. I trembled each time I heard the rattle of his keys near the door and I had taken to locking the kids in their rooms at night for fear that he would harm them. Now looking back I don´t understand how I could have been so stupid and not have reacted so much earlier, why I thought my story would be different from that of so many others."

"I don´t know how long I intended on deceiving myself. I had nowhere to go, my parents were not well off, turning up at their doorstep with two small children would have put them in a very difficult position, I didn´t stop to think that they would rather have had nothing to eat themselves than see me dead. One day while I was cleaning the house and listening to the news, it was announced that domestic violence had claimed one more victim. I sat down to watch it and I saw a body being wheeled out of a house on a stretcher while a small child was crying and trying to hold on to a lifeless hand. At the same time, two police men were escorting a handcuffed man out of the building. At that precise moment, the scales finally fell from my eyes, that was going to be me, one day he would go too far and kill me in front of my children, I would be responsible for them having that image for ever on their minds. The newscaster urged all women going through the same situation to call a number that was on screen, I found myself reaching out for the phone and though my fingers were dithering, I was actually dialling the number. I was told to leave my house immediately with my children and our ID cards. I picked them both up and left what had not been my home for such a long time, I left with nothing, just like when I first got there, except that then, I had hope and a future. For everyone who is going through something similar, he is not going to change, he will kill you or worse, one of your children and there is no coming back from that."

As she utters those last words, the image on the screen changes to one of two smiling children, at that moment I feel the bile come up my throat, I get up quickly and rush out of the room blinded by the tears that had poured from my eyes as soon as I saw the wedding photograph. I stumble into the rest rooms just in time, just before everything I had just eaten came out of my mouth again. I am shaking and feel physically ill because I have now realised that I have married a psychopath and that he is more than likely going to kill me. Like Julia, I have succeeded in deluding myself into believing that things have changed, that there is a reason for all that has happened, but that it is now over. I feel a chill go through me as I straighten up from the toilet bowl, I remember that when I glanced at him as we all listened to her story, he was smiling.

NINE

BALOU

The group that comes back that evening is silent, they left in such high spirits earlier on, I wonder what has happened? Rosario and her mother enter the house holding each other and the men retire to their rooms. Rosario comes looking for me and she holds me and cries for hours while we sit on the sofa in darkness. I have no idea what has taken place but it feels like something has broken in her. She is shivering whilst sobbing at the same time, in such a way like I have never heard her before and I have seen her cry many times. We stay curled up on a sofa in the parlour all night; I didn't leave her side, except when I had to use the litter tray and also have something to eat.

The next day Rosario looks drained, I feel that it's only when she is with me that can she show her true emotions; when her parents come down for breakfast she smiles at them and speaks to them as if everything is perfect. I stay around should she need me. It makes me extremely uncomfortable when something is going on and I don´t know what it is. I follow her father as he goes out into the garden, I have noticed that he is the only one that isn´t convinced about my adorable self and I decide that I need to win him over. I am a vain creature and I can´t stand the thought that there is someone that does not care much for me. He is standing under a tree smoking his pipe, Rosario does not allow him to smoke in the house, she says everything smells horrible and that it takes ages to get rid of the odour from the curtains and furniture; she is very sensitive to smells. I rub myself against his boots and look up at him in what I assume is my most endearing expression and he looks down at me, I hear him mutter "little devil". I have excellent hearing and I start to purr. He takes his pipe out of his mouth and laughs out loud as he bends down to scratch my head and I close my eyes in appreciation. I then walk away with my head held high, I´ve got what I went for, better leave him wanting more so he can come and find me. I don´t turn around but I know he is watching me. A short time later when he comes into the house, he enters the kitchen where I have settled down on my favourite high stool while I watch Adela work her magic. There are lovely smells coming out from the pot she is stirring. I am hopeful that something might come my way.

"There you are, leave the women alone, your place is with me, let's go and run outside I want to see some movement from that round body of yours."

After letting out an anguished meow as I feel myself being lifted up from my comfortable spot I am taken outside and unceremoniously deposited on the lawn. I start looking back and calculating how many seconds it will take me to get back to the door when out of the corner of my eye I see him take something from a pocket in his coat; I decide to see what it is before taking off and to my great delight I discover it's the laser mouse. I assume the position in readiness to catch the little red light as soon as it appears. We have a great time with me running all over the place and soon we have an audience; Juan, Rosario and her mother are laughing and point me in the direction of the light. I don't know why, I can see it perfectly.

"Yep, he can run" says my human grandfather, as he goes into the house while his wife picks me up. This family definitely has a thing for constantly lifting me from the ground and ignoring my attempts to get down. Can't they read my facial expressions?

I'm glad that "Cold Eyes" had to leave very early for the office; he would have spoilt the day for us. It's noticeable that Rosario is less tense too, although I have caught her with a far away expression on her face on numerous occasions. But, all good things come to an end when he comes home for lunch. I hear him say that he escaped from work so he could spend some "quality" time with the family, he smiles while he says this and I notice his wife quickly looks away.

After lunch, I bite Javier. I am on my way to sit by the side of Rosario's father, I have grown accustomed to him in the short while he has been with us; when that evil man picks me up, he is trying to pretend in front of everybody that we are on good terms, but I am not going to give that impression at all, if he wasn't responsible for his wife's unhappiness last night, then why was he not by her side comforting her? So I sink my teeth into his arm and I draw blood. He yells and lets go of me, I land on my feet and put some distance between us, hiding behind the man I now consider my grandfather. He looks at me in fury, but also with impotence as I know he wouldn't dare touch me in front of our guests. Rosario goes to get the first aid kit whilst telling him that he must have handled me too roughly as I had never done that before.

"It seems Balou does not like you, I notice he is never by your side and now he bites you. Javier, what dark secrets are you hiding from us?" says her father, laughing while he pats my head.

"Oh you know cats, they choose their people and tend to ignore the rest of the household, but there is really no bad blood between us" replies the cynical man, while looking at me with anything but love.

In the evening, our guests leave; it is with sadness that Rosario and I stand together outside the house as we watch the car disappear through the gates...

I go back to the kitchen, to the loving arms of cook, she complains that as we had visitors, she has seen very little of me. I stay awhile to reassure her and also because she has just given me a raw chicken wing which I love to chew, chase around the kitchen floor and eventually destroy. Suddenly we hear a loud noise and a scream, I practically jump out of my skin and rush after Adela and Juan, who had just come into the kitchen for a glass of water. We all run up the stairs; I get there a fraction of a second before the other two, proving once again, that my size does not limit my sprinting abilities.

The scene before my eyes is horrific, Rosario is lying on the floor and Javier is punching her, there is blood all over her face and on the white shirt she is wearing. She is trying to push herself away by heaving her legs but he has her pinned down. I don´t think about it twice and throw myself at his face, claws and teeth out. He screams and lets go of her as I drag my claws across the whole length of his face, he flings me across the room and I hit the wall... Meanwhile, Juan rushes to lift Rosario up from the floor; he succeeds, with the help of Adela. I am able to land on my feet; I arch my back and hiss, ready to go again... Javier wipes his face with his hands, he looks down and sees the blood and starts advancing towards me, his intentions are very clear so I prepare myself for battle. I decide to go for his ankles and bite away, it is the only idea that comes to my head, I hiss again and emit what I hope is a blood curling howl but I have no idea what effect it will have as I haven´t been able to practice it before.

"I have borne all forms of abuse from you but if you ever, hear me well... if you ever lay a finger on my cat again, I will make sure that I destroy you and that on your way down you will take your entire family with you."

Everyone else in the room stands still whilst Javier and a bloody Rosario stare at each other. He must have seen something in the one eye that she can manage to keep half-open as he turns around and walks away. At that precise moment, Rosario collapses; Juan picks her up and takes her away. Marco and Marylin that had come in late start picking up things that had been knocked over during the "fight". Marco stops to pat me and I growl at him, there is so much tension in me that I feel the need to attack and punish something or someone. Adela is crying and calling me to go to her, I can tell that she is scared by what has just happened and seeing me like this. I see her legs shake as she slowly slides down and sits on the floor. I stand with my back arched, I can feel all the hairs on my body stand on end and I back away from everyone. I hear a strange sound coming out from me, it takes me a few seconds to realise that I am hissing at them and that they are scared of coming any closer. With an angry and what sounds like an eternal meow I blindly race out of the room, leaving the remnants of the disaster behind me.

TEN

ROSARIO

My parents leave and I feel a physical pain as I watch the car drive out of view. These last few days, I have felt so safe in their presence, like nothing could happen to me because they were protecting me, just like they did when I was a child. I watch Balou retreat into the kitchen, he is such a clever and happy little cat, he won my father over, something I thought would never happen, my father's animal passion lies with horses. He is so proud of the ones he has and spends hours grooming them when he has the time. He has won various prizes at exhibitions and fairs, and on several occasions he has even been approached to sell one or two that have caught the fancy of someone, they have offered exorbitant amounts for them, my father has always refused because he says that he does not trust anyone else to treat them the way he does. On my wedding day, two of the "apples of his eyes" led our chariot to the cathedral through the streets of Sevilla, I could tell that my father was proud that his first daughter was getting married, but also that his beautiful horses had played their role that day to perfection too. I caught him reading the newspaper with the cat by his side, he scratched Balou´s head and chin in an absent-minded manner, I laugh when I see the way Balou places the part of his anatomy he wants my father to scratch within his reach. I shiver as I think that I am once again alone with Javier and my resolve to leave him after seeing my life pass before my eyes last night has weakened. In broad daylight, I tell myself that things are not so serious and that the women that told their story the evening before had let things go too far, that the smile I had seen on his face as he listened to Julia was just a figment of my imagination. I need to take a step back and re-evaluate my situation. Hasty decisions are never good.

I go up into my study to take a book to read, I´m starting to get a headache and intend to go to bed early, when Javier walks in. We have barely spoken a word since the evening before.

"I think you need to stop working with abused women."

--

"What?"

"I can say it louder but not any clearer, you need to inform them that you are no longer able to look after their project in your Foundation."

"Why would I do that?"

"Because it seems to be something that affects you, yesterday you succeeded in making a fool of yourself and me in the process. Good thing that the press saw it as being in touch with the pain of that stupid woman."

I drop the book I'm holding while I look at him in amazement and I see that he is completely serious.

"I am not going to do that, thanks to what we are doing, women like that have an option. Are you afraid that through my involvement, somehow people might get to see the kind of a man you really are?"

Javier is advancing towards me and I move quickly behind the desk to try and put some physical distance between us, in my haste I collide with a chair and knock it over on to the floor.

"And what am I? There is absolutely nothing wrong with me, except the fact that I married a woman who brings out the worst in me. Ask anyone, I am a wonderful person.

We should clarify something this very moment, just in case the event yesterday has put some kind of stupid idea in that empty head of yours, the only way you will ever leave me is in a pine box, feet first. Yes, I read minds too."

He is now in front of the desk and I realise I have made a horrible mistake as I have nowhere to run to; there is only the wall behind me. I wonder if I can pretend to run in one direction and then go the other way. Maybe it is the only chance I have of escaping, from the look in his eyes I know the way this conversation is going to end. I do just that but I´m not fast enough as Javier catches hold of my arm and twists it behind my back, I let out a scream of pain as I fall to the ground on my knees and he starts hitting me. This time he doesn´t bother avoiding my face and my hands offer me no protection from him, he punches me in my stomach, chest, face, I can´t fight him off, I start finding it difficult to breathe. Suddenly, I feel something fly past me and I hear a horrible meow as Javier swears and curses. Two strong arms lift me from the ground, I hear Balou hiss. I´m finding it difficult to open one of my eyes, I can only see from the other and even that one does not open completely. I feel pain as I manage to open it a little, I see the man I made the mistake of marrying walking menacingly towards my Balou. In that instant something snaps inside of me, just the thought that he might harm him makes me stand up to him. I don´t know how, but I find the strength to threaten him, I can't see myself but the faces of my staff tell me that this time it's different, Javier must have sensed something in my voice because he turns around from his intent of attacking Balou and walks away.

My legs give away under me and Juan takes me to my room, Marylin comes in quickly with the first aid kit but as she looks at me I can see she doesn't know where to start. The pain is unbearable. After a short while Adela comes in crying because Balou has run off and she thinks he might have lost his mind. He didn't seem to recognise any of them and was hissing all the time. She sees me and starts crying even harder; I imagine I must have taken a beating worse than I thought I had. She says she has to call the doctor but I ask her not to do that, I can't have anyone see me this way.

"*Señora*[4], I have to. I'm afraid for your eye, your lip is also badly cut, you are bleeding and I fear you might have some internal injuries. Someone needs to make sure that you are ok. It's not normal that you should flinch in such pain each time anyone tries to touch you."

I ask her to bring my phone book and tell her to call a number. Half an hour later, Gonzalo Altamira walks

---

[4] Madam in Spanish, original language everything in the novel is spoken in.

in. We´ve known each other since we were kids, our families were very close and years later, we met again at a function in Madrid. He is a doctor, he stares at me when he comes in and starts working immediately. I must be really bad if he hasn´t bothered asking me any questions. One hour later, I´m full of pain killers and have received several stitches. He finally finishes and goes into the bathroom to wash his hands.

"What happened?"

"I went into my study and surprised someone trying to open my safe. He attacked me and ran away. Juan and Adela found me unconscious."

"Have you alerted the police? Why did you call me instead of going directly to the hospital?"

"I really don´t want this to be known, you know how it is, the slightest news fills up hours and hours of gossip programmes and someone will somehow get a photograph of my face, I don´t want to worry Javier and my family."

"This does not just seem like some random attack, one would just think the assailant would just push you away in order to escape. He has beaten you quite badly. I need to get you to the hospital and do some x-rays, I suspect you might have broken ribs as you have such difficulty breathing. Where is your husband?"

"He isn't back from his work trip yet. Gonzalo, you need to treat me here, whatever it takes and whatever you need, I'll pay for it."

"You really need to report this; I have to do so too, the law requires it of me when such serious injuries are sustained. It's not about the money, it's about giving you the best treatment I can and I need equipment I don't have here. Are you sure it wasn't someone you know?"

"I didn't see his face, he wore a mask"

We argue some more as I beg him not to alert the authorities, he must finally have sensed my anguish because he said he wouldn't and that he would come back to check on me the next day. When he leaves, I sense Adela and Juan are disapproving of what I have just done, but I start falling asleep and it suddenly doesn't matter anymore.

I spend the next few days in bed as I ache all over, Gonzalo comes in daily to see me and dress my wounds. I don't see Javier, but my staff are constantly in and out of the room and I guess he doesn't want to venture in, not knowing if anyone will go for him. I call the office and tell

Pilar that I have come down with the 'flu' and the doctor has ordered bed rest.

I start planning how to escape out of a situation that I have let go on for too long, because this time it had been different, I sensed Javier would not have stopped if the others had not come rushing in and Balou had not attacked him.

ELEVEN

ROSARIO

Three days after the incident, my door opens and Concha, my mother in law comes in. She puts her hand over her mouth in shock when she sees me; I guess I still look as if a bulldozer has just driven over me. She has the bad habit of coming to my house unannounced and when I least expect it. The last person I want to see at this point in time is the woman who gave birth to the monster who did this to me!

"What has happened to you? Was this Javier?"

I stare at her as she sits down and starts sobbing, while she buries her face in her hands.

"I guess you don't need an answer to your question, but I do want to know why you immediately jumped to the conclusion that your son is responsible for what you see in front of you. I know nobody in this house would have volunteered that information."

"We thought he had changed and that part of him was dead and buried."

"Changed from what?"

"Javier has always had a vicious temper, from when he was a child. He used to fly into a rage and smash things. He would suddenly lose control for the most insignificant reasons. We took him to a psychologist when he was growing up and after sometime in therapy, he said he was fine and didn't need to go anymore. Until a few years ago…"

"What happened?"

"He was dating a girl, they hadn't known each other long. One night they had an argument and he beat her up, very badly. It happened in our house in the country. The maid called to inform us and we rushed there to find the girl unconscious. When she came to and after she had been seen by a trusted doctor friend of ours, my husband offered her a very substantial sum of money so she could disappear. She was asked to sign a confidentiality agreement saying she could never speak about what happened."

As I listen to her I grow more and more angry, not able to believe the words I'm hearing. If she had been honest with me when we first met, I would have walked away from him and we wouldn't be where we are today. All this could have been avoided.

"How can you sit there and cry when you are responsible for what your son has done to me? Why did you encourage the relationship?"

"I really thought that it had been an isolated incident as we never learnt of anything similar happening and he seemed so happy with you. I tried to keep an eye on things and come by from time to time to see if anything was wrong but until today, everything seemed so perfect."

"You must have known deep down the kind of sick and twisted mind that your son has, but it seems I was too good a deal to let pass by. With the merging of our two families, you struck gold. It just didn't matter to you what might happen to me."

She starts shaking her head as I speak and we both look at each other. At this point I am shaking with anger as I can't believe that she endangered my life in such a way.

"We really thought you were both happy, I had no idea what was going on. What are you going to do now?"

"Well as you decided to withhold such important information from me, I'm sure you understand that I have no desire to share my plans with you."

"Please, please don't go to the police, or tell your family, even though you must hate Javier now and you have every right to do so, he is a good man and this could ruin him."

"Are you going to try to pay me off too? Just how much do you think my silence is worth? I can't believe you, even now, all you think about is your reputation. Well, I'm going to let you into a little secret... I couldn't care less what happens to your good family name or whether Javier spends some well deserved time in jail. I can't get up to show you out but please leave. I really don't want to have anything more to do with any of you and I certainly have no desire to continue with this conversation."

"I have loved you and treated you like a daughter..."

"Are you serious? If you knew your daughter was dating a dangerous and violent man, would you have just let her go ahead? If it was the other way round and I was yours, would you have let me marry Javier?"

"No."

She looks surprised at the answer she has just given me and I stare at her feeling that for the first time since we started the conversation, she is being honest. I look towards the wall and a few minutes later, I feel her leave the room. As soon as I get better, I'm getting out of the house, I don't need to receive any more warnings before taking the decision.

Balou had got down from the bed to sniff Concha's bag as he normally does when he comes in contact with one. As soon as she leaves, he jumps back up on to the bed and comes towards my face, I cry out in pain as he sinks his paws in my stomach but I don't push him away as he is purring and I don't want him to leave. He rubs his nose against mine and decides that my body is the best place to settle on for a siesta. He is becoming quite big and heavy and every nerve in my body is screaming in pain but for some strange reason, I'd rather he stayed with me than push him away.

After he ran away following the incident, he stayed in hiding for a day, nobody knew where he was and I was terribly worried. I was on pain killers for the pain and also on medication for the high fever I had developed; I was delirious and kept calling him in my sleep. Everyone in the house was looking for him. A day later he walked into the room and sat near the threshold looking up at me for some time. I started crying when I saw him, I was afraid that something in him had snapped from the shock of what had happened and he wasn't able to recognise me. I couldn't stand the thought of that happening, he is all I have in this house. Suddenly he jumped on the bed and started smelling me as he came closer to my face, stopping just a few inches from it, all the time sniffing. I think that with all the ointment I had on my face and eyes he wasn't able to identify my scent as something familiar to him. I held my breath wondering what his next move would be; his big yellow eyes were fixed on me. He inched closer and closer and started cleaning my face. His tongue was rough and raspy and every single time it came into contact with my skin, I saw stars! It seemed a very important task to him but I was afraid that what he was ingesting could be toxic so I lifted my arm to stroke and distract him. Every movement I made sent a searing pain through my body. Javier had punched me everywhere and the medication just wasn't enough to mask my body's reaction to that. Balou started grooming my hand instead; he has practically not left my side since then.

The nights are horrible, I can't sleep as I keep listening for Javier's footsteps in the long corridors. When I do manage to doze off, my dreams are filled with the events that occurred and I feel the pain of each blow again and again. Adela has stayed in the room next to mine since the incident, I told her it wasn't necessary but she said she couldn´t go to her house and come back the next day to find me dead and that as I didn´t want to hire a nurse, she would tend to me until I was on my feet again. So she checks on me throughout the night, she knows I can´t sleep so she sits by my side for a long time. It´s funny how even though I have always known that she was a good worker and a good person, I had not really stopped to actually talk to her and get to know her. Yet, she has barely left my side. Now, I know that she is a widow with two married daughters who decided to put her cooking skills to good use after her husband´s death. I can hardly keep anything down these days, the medication along with the state of my nerves have upset my stomach and I keep throwing up, but throughout it all Adela doesn´t leave my side. She keeps making different soups and spoon-feeding me, because if she doesn't, she knows that each time she comes into the room, the food will be exactly how she left it, untouched.

She has not spoken to me about what happened, I know that she does not want to cross the line between employee and boss. I am so ashamed that she had to witness what happened, I don´t know what to say to her, where to begin or how to excuse that I let that happen, yet I feel that I have to say something.

"He wasn´t always like this."

She stops straightening the bed sheets and looks up at me for a moment, then she continues what she is doing, I really don´t know what to say after that. This is the first time after the visit from Javier´s mother that I feel like I can admit to someone else that my life is far from perfect.

"Most of them weren´t like that at first. I don´t know why they decide it´s fine to beat to a pulp someone much weaker than themselves, but they do, some say it´s jealousy, insecurity, possessiveness... I have known for some time that things were not right; sleeping in separate bedrooms and hardly speaking to each other, but I had no idea it had reached this point. I have lost all my respect for that man. This is no marriage, I was married for thirty years before I lost my *Paco*[5] to cancer, we quarreled, we argued, we got annoyed with each other, sometimes we went for days without speaking, but never, ever, did he raise his hand to me. When someone does that, it is because they have lost every single ounce of love and respect for you. If we had not been there, he would have killed you. Please, please leave him. Don´t let him be the one to take you out of this world."

"It has never been this bad, I thought it was my fault, that I triggered that response in him and after sometime I lost the will to fight anymore or want to walk

---

[5] Popular short form of the name Francisco.

away, but somehow, having Balou has made me want to leave before he kills us both. In everyone else's eyes I know he is just a cat, but he has made me laugh again, when I saw Javier fling him across the room and go for him, I forgot the pain I was in, I really don't remember how I even got up from the floor, but I couldn't let him harm him."

"He isn't just an insignificant cat, we love him dearly and he protected you with his life, when it happened my first move was to try to calm him instead of coming to you first. Later, when I thought about all the events that occurred I was surprised at this. I haven't seen that man since it happened, he got into his car and drove off, I hope never to return, but that cat paces up and down the corridors and is ready for battle should he be called upon. I was shocked at the way he reacted, I've heard of dogs doing that but never cats. It goes to show that one can never measure the devotion these little creatures show for those that love them. He has barely left your side since it happened and that for him must be a great sacrifice because he loves occupying the front row in the kitchen."

We both look at Balou who is biting one of my slippers and "bunny" kicking them with his hind legs, I smile at his round body and the concentration he is putting into this task. He takes everything he does very seriously, my little black panther.

TWELVE

BALOU

I run and run after leaving that room where everything had happened, I can't seem to stop. After some time I go into one of the spare rooms and hide under the bed, I get to the far end where no one can reach me. I hear my name being called out repeatedly but I'm not going out again, not until I get rid of the fear and anger that man has instilled in me. I knew I disliked him intensely and that he was not a good person, but today I saw something else in his eyes, he is evil, there is absolutely nothing good in him and he has the power to do much harm. My first impulse is to run away and never come back, I start to move towards the door, everything is quiet, now is my chance. I stand in the corridor and start moving towards the stairs and then an image of Rosario on the floor with her hands covering her face while that man hit her repeatedly comes to mind. I stop in my tracks, I can't leave her behind. He will come back to finish what he started, I'm not stupid, I know that I'm no match for him but I can try my best. I hear better than she does, I can somehow warn her when he is approaching. I retrace my steps and go back under the bed. I'm exhausted and I need to sleep, but today, it's going to be with one eye open. It's ironic that sometimes the real beasts are two-legged creatures who are supposed to be the least primitive in the animal kingdom, yet it is in them that we find the most ugly emotions.

The next morning Juan calls out to me, I hear him moving from room to room, then he comes in the one I am in. He goes into the bathroom and makes sounds to draw me out. He looks under the bed and even though it is dark, it is an unused room and the curtains are not drawn, he can see my eyes. I hear him shout that he has found me and Adela, Marylin and Marcos run into the room, they all call out to me and hold out their hands but I don't really feel like coming out into so much space, unprotected. I feel safe where I am. Adela tells me that the wicked man has gone, I can come out, but I stay put. She then comes back with a plate and leaves it on the floor, the strong smell of cooked chicken reaches my delicate nose and my stomach rumbles. I haven't eaten and I am hungry. They leave the room and I wait a while longer, just to make sure that they are gone. Then I slowly come out from my hiding place and begin to eat. The door is open and I watch the hall as I eat. I hear footsteps and go back under the bed; Juan sits down on the floor in the hall, facing the door. I come out again to finish eating and when I´m done, I automatically do what any cat with a minimum etiquette would do, clean myself. When I finish, I look up and Juan and Adela are there, still sitting on the floor, I walk towards the cook´s outstretched hand, they both stroke my head and under my chin. When they finally leave I take a tour of the house, to be sure that we are really alone as I have been assured. I finally stop in front of the open door of Rosario´s room and I look at her, I can barely recognise her, one of her eyes is completely shut and so swollen, her face has various shades of colours. She calls my name, I find myself unable to move while I try to find the woman I´ve come to love , she is now the broken human being who is lying on the bed. Finally I decide that the least I can do is give her a good wash. As I get close to here, I notice that there is a very strong and not very pleasant smell emanating from her, another reason for a good grooming session. So I start working, she soon offers me her hand to continue, I really don´t mind where I start from, there is a lot of ground to cover.

I hardly ever leave her side as I have to be sure I will be there when "Evil Incarnate" returns, also, I can see that

--

each movement she makes is extremely painful for her and it seems my presence gives her some comfort. From time to time, I go out to eat as I need my strength in order to defend the fort. While I move around the house, I keep an eye open for signs of Javier but he is nowhere to be seen. I really hope we've seen the last of him, maybe he saw in our faces how much we all hate him and he got scared of what we might do to him. I know this is just wishful thinking on my part, as worms always find a way of returning to the rotten apple.

Rosario does not have visitors, that is apart from the man who comes in daily to check on her and treat her wounds, he argues with her each time he comes, telling her she has to report the incident, she has given him a completely different version of what happened, he also asks for Javier and he is told that he is away on business. I sense that he is worried, he says that she has a fever that doesn't seem to be going away. Both Adela and I stay close by when he comes, we want her on her feet as soon as possible but it doesn't appear to be happening, I think she really doesn't feel like doing that, she sleeps a lot and when she is awake, she spends all her time just staring at the wall. I perk up when a tall, thin, white-haired woman comes into the room, I'm hoping that something good is about to happen but as soon as Rosario sets eyes on her, I feel her stiffen and my hopes are dashed.

So this is Javier's mother. I did wonder before meeting her what kind of person was responsible for punishing the world with his presence and even though she seemed to present a sort of unapproachable front, I sense a great fear and sadness in her. She tries to hold a conversation with Rosario but to no avail, she is asked to leave almost as soon as she arrives, it is clear that she is blamed for what has happened too.

I spend the next two days following the same routine and barely leaving Rosario's side, at least her doctor friend seems a bit happier with her progress, he has stopped arguing with her, but it is obvious that he disapproves of her unwillingness to talk and he feels helpless at not being able to do anything about it himself either.

I'm indulging in one of my daily naps when I hear the sound of footsteps, suddenly, I spring to my feet, my back arched, I start hissing and growling as at that precise moment, the cause of all our troubles walks in.

--

THIRTEEN

ROSARIO

I have a splitting headache and the pills I have taken don't seem to be working; it feels like someone is hitting my head with a hammer. I close my eyes as Adela applies a cold compress to my forehead, she leaves the room to get me some tea in case I need a sip, she tells me. Just as I'm finally drifting off to sleep, I feel Balou make a sudden movement and I hear him growl. I open one eye and struggle to sit up as there in front of me is Javier. I look around wildly for something with which to defend myself as he probably has come back to finish what he started; I feel the fear build up quickly inside of me. There is nothing, nothing that can be of help to me. He comes near the bed and looks down at me while he strokes my face with his hand.

Immediately Juan and Adela rush into the room, they stand tense while they watch Javier who takes his hand back as soon as they come in. Balou has not stopped hissing and I'm holding on to him with all my strength as I don't want Javier to fling him against the wall again.

I am trembling, I have no idea where the man I married has disappeared to and exactly what the one now standing in front of me is capable of? I know he has several guns which he uses when he goes hunting with his friends, in my mind there is a clear image of all of us on the floor, lifeless, in a pool of blood.

Juan and Adela stand as close to me as possible, Balou has climbed on the dresser and from all indications, is ready to pounce on him. I'm guessing he will be going for that handsome face that is now marked from the scratches Balou gave him before, for a second, both man and beast lock eyes, they stare intently at each other, until Javier looks at me and holds up his hands.

"I come in peace... I can assure you all that the last thing that is going to happen is a repeat of the incident last week."

"Incident?"

I look at Adela, who is looking at Javier with rage whilst standing with her arms akimbo.

"You call beating your wife almost to death an incident? You actually have the nerve to stand there and calmly say that. You are definitely more evil than I initially thought you were. You caught us by surprise last time but now we are ready and I can assure you that this time, it can only end one way."

Javier looks at her with a raised eyebrow and then he gazes at me, I wonder whether we can take him down. I'm not much use as I still ache all over but Juan is tall and young, he is strong so it might be an even fight and Adela seems to be ready for battle, she is a heavy woman, which is probably a good attribute for fighting.

"Yes, you are right, in my mind I have downplayed everything that happened as I just can't believe what took place here, I just can't comprehend what I did."

His voice breaks off and he stops talking while his eyes well up. I can't believe what I'm seeing, towering and intimidating Javier is crying. I look towards Adela who still has the same body posture, only now she is tapping her left foot on the floor with visible impatience and anger.

"Save those crocodile tears for someone who doesn´t know you or who actually cares. This is not a one-off event; this has happened too many times before, do you think you can come in here and try to deceive us? We suspected something was off with you, we just never imagined you were systematically torturing your wife and if there is something that I can´t accept, is a man who takes advantage of his strength to prey on the weak. She is not alone; we will protect her with our lives if we have to. You have already spent ten minutes too many here, leave before we call the police, or stay so we can call them and end all this, I actually prefer the second option."

Juan and I are silent while Adela continues, she is practically shouting at the end of her speech and by the way she is breathing you can tell she is really angry. I feel I need to find my voice and back her up, even though I have no strength to fight or argue, I´m shocked as a small part of me, the small part that is past caring wants him to just end it all. I´m so tired, I can´t keep living with fear, not knowing which day will be my last, if I let him kill me then I will be free of all this, I shake away that horrible thought and try to stay focused.

"Javier, please leave. This marriage is over and the only reason that I didn't call the police is because I couldn't bear my parents knowing the hell you've put me through these past years."

"I just need to speak to you a few minutes alone and after that I promise I will leave."

"No."

We all look at Juan who had been quiet till that moment, he is looking directly at Javier, gone from his eyes is the respect with which he used to look at him, it is no longer an employee speaking to his employer. It is a battle of equals. I decide to get it over with as this could drag on eternally.

"Adela and Juan I can´t thank you enough for standing by me the way you have but the sooner we do this, the sooner I get this man out of my life. I will speak to him and the door will be open. Juan go to his study and get one of his guns, you will find the corresponding bullets in the third drawer of his desk. If you see anything that makes you fear for my life, just shoot him."

Javier looks in amazement at me when I say this, but Juan then leaves the room to do what I have asked of him while Adela is still standing between us. I know she strongly disapproves of the fact that he has still not been physically thrown out; even though we have become quite close and she knows much more about me, there is still a line that she won´t cross and she will respect my wishes. Juan comes in with a rifle and they both stand in the hall leaving the door open, I look at the man in front of me, I want him to say what he has come to say and then just go. I have had time to really think and much as I´m afraid of taking the step of leaving him, I know that I will end up dead if I don´t. Javier sits down on the sofa across the room from me, he keeps rubbing his hands which I now notice are shaking.

"I came here with a speech prepared in my mind, some form of explanation but seeing you and what I have done...There are just no words that can defend my actions. I can´t apologise for this."

He is referring to my bruises which have gone through all the possible colours of the rainbow and they are now in the green stage, if there was anything to laugh at from this whole situation, it´s that I probably look just like what someone from Mars would. No need for paint or make up. I honestly have no idea what he expects me to say at this point. Does he want me to say that all is just forgiven and forgotten?

"I don´t expect your forgiveness, I have gone way beyond forgetting a birthday..."

"You speak as if, this has happened just once, I´ve actually lost count of the number of times your fists have rained down on me, how you've reduced me to a trembling, frightened person, with an extremely low self-esteem. You have robbed me of the will to live or the ability to have hopes and dreams because I can't seem to see beyond the day I'm living in, you have isolated me completely from the world and the people I love most. Exactly which of these things would you like me to forgive you for?"

I'm surprised at myself as I say this as I'm not someone who is prone to feeling rage, but I realise that as I see him before me, looking vulnerable, I feel the need to tell him for the first time since all this started, exactly what he has done to me. He remains silent while he listens to me, just staring at me... this makes me feel even more angry. He owes me an explanation; I need to know what happened, why things went so wrong? I sometimes feel that when I touch rock bottom it is somehow my own entire fault. With all the emotions that are constantly overwhelming me, guilt is mixed in there with them.

"I really don't know what happened last week or on the previous occasions. I feel a rage build up inside me and before I know it, I lash out. The other day, I left here horrified at myself, I could have killed you and although you might find this impossible to believe at the moment, you are the most important person in my life."

"Yet, anyone who has looked through a key hole on our last five years would laugh out loud at what you have just said. But, we are only wasting time, I actually have to be grateful to you, I needed something to make me open my eyes and see just how bad our situation is. It´s unsustainable, I should never have made excuses for you or allowed this to go on and this is my fault. I should have left the first time you disrespected me. For the sake of our families, I will cite irreconcilable differences and I don´t want any of your money or assets. I just never, ever, want to see you again."

"I hear everything you are saying and I´m ready to give you what you want but I need a little bit of time. I´m seeing someone to help me try and put everything right, I need you not to disappear from my life at the moment because even though I have no right to ask you, I really need you in order to be able get through this. I just don´t know how to come back from what I have become on my own."

FOURTEEN

BALOU

I have a lot of qualities and abilities, really quite a lot, but sadly speech is not one of them. Had I been able to talk, I would have said, no, screamed for Rosario to run away from "Evil Incarnate." As I listen to all he has to say, I just can't understand how she does not see that he is only buying time, he is a monster, he does not feel any remorse. Just like me when I'm being scolded for scratching the leather sofa in the hall, do I understand that I'm being scolded? Yes. Do I care? No. I don't feel I'm doing anything wrong, it's fun, it's in my way, so I do it. I see the same things in him, why can't she see it? He does not feel sorry for hurting her, to him, it all comes so natural; he feels absolutely no guilt for his actions.

They agree that he will live in the pool house, which for me isn't punishment as it is massive and he has every single comfort he could possible need there. It just seems like he is getting away with everything, all I can do is look from one to the other while they make arrangements without understanding what is happening, she had started the conversation and negotiations with so much strength and as the minutes went by, I see her slowly fade away and lose the will to fight. It is such a subtle change but I see it, so does he because he presses on until he gets exactly what he wants. He is an expert manipulator, he knows exactly which buttons to push to get what he wants and now, he needs to buy time. For what? For nothing good, his ideas are just never beneficial to anyone around him. He has a plan, I know it.

So now I have to keep interrupting my much needed siestas in order to keep an eye on things, he doesn't come into the house and actually spends a lot of time away, he leaves in the morning and I hear his car come back late at night. I just go and make sure that he is locked in for the night. There is now a cat flap that was installed in the glass kitchen door, which allows me to go out when I want, so I make my rounds and peer through his windows, just to be sure that he is where he is supposed to be.

--

When Juan and Adela found out that he was staying on, they were livid. Adela told Rosario that she was making a mistake, that he was not to be trusted and for a split second I saw her hesitate and I had the hope that she would see just how insane what she was doing was, but she thanked Adela and said she was doing what was right. Right? We must have very different definitions of that word because no matter which angle I look at things from I just can´t see anything good about this plan. She presses her some more but we both see in Rosario´s face that she is not going back on her decision, so she leaves the room with an anger that I know she can´t express in words to her employer. I know her well, when she is in the kitchen and something goes wrong, she uses a lot of swear words that I sense some of which she is itching to use now.

Later when I go to the kitchen to receive my daily dose of cuddles and words of love, my presence interrupts a meeting between all the staff, they look at me as I come in but as I´m just the cat, they carry on. They are all seated around the big table where they normally have lunch and breakfast.

"We have to protect her and make sure we have him always in sight when he is on the premises. I know that she is only letting him stay here because of something he said to her. We had talked about it, we made plans. She was going to leave him. We had even looked at a few properties online that were for sale as it was going to be a fresh start for all of us, now a few minutes with that man and everything is on hold."

They all look at Adela when she says this, shifting their attention from their half drunken cups of coffee. Marcos nods his head.

"We need this job because we are sending money to our families in the Philippines, he was the one that employed both Marylin and I but if I see anything that even remotely resembles the horror of two weeks ago, I'm calling the police. I don't care if I lose my job, I can't sit back and watch a woman be treated in such an inhumane way, even animals are treated much better, can you imagine, people are fined and some even get jail sentences for animal cruelty, yet this man is just getting away with everything. The days of enforced silence are over, she does not have to be afraid to speak out or hide behind the doors of this house. I know what is wrong, he is using the fact that in their case it would be made public and the *señora* does not want anyone to know her business. He has got someone to come in and clean the pool house which is good as I don't know how I would have kept the disdain I feel for him showing on my face had I been ordered to do so."

I look at Marcos as he speaks and wonder what he is talking about as his face normally does not register any form of emotion, I can never tell what he is feeling by looking at him, I have never heard him raise his voice in all the time I have been here. Not like the rest of them have done, especially when I'm doing something they consider inappropriate, but I also know how to read body language and from the tone of his words and posture I feel his anger.

I jump on to my special stool which is close to the kitchen table so I can somehow feel part of this vigilante group. I suddenly don't feel so alone, there are others watching over her, others that can do so much more than I can, that can match strength with strength. I look at Juan, he is almost as tall as Javier so this means that if the need arose, he could tackle him and with the help of the rest of us, we could bring him down. After all, even though he is incredibly destructive and strong, he is just one man.

"And let's not forget that we have our little hero here, who disregarding his own safety went for his face. I have to say it gave me great pleasure to still see the scratches on Javier's face when he came in, for that, you are getting a piece of *Jamón*."

I immediately perk up as I hear her words and look towards the counter where she keeps the meat she cuts

---

[6] Cured ham, one of the most popular foods used for tapas or aperitifs in Spain.

daily. The rest laugh as they see my eagerness and Marylin who is closest to me, pats my head. Adela puts two pieces on the table and I quickly transport myself there and do my special type of magic, I make them disappear.

The rest soon disband and go back to their daily chores, I debate who to follow and I finally decide to stay with the warmth of both the kitchen and Adela, especially as when she cooks, something always comes my way. Rosario has asked her not to feed me human food as she orders mine especially for me; she couldn´t buy good quality cat food in the shops here. She spent time researching and she explained to Adela that some things she put in their food when cooking were harmful for me, but Adela just laughed and told me that cats had always been fed from the kitchen left over's and that she was sure that she was partly responsible for the great shine of my coat. So I´m okay with keeping our little secret, she´s happy, I´m happy...

I hear footsteps coming down the stairs and I leave my comfortable spot beside Adela to investigate, I come across Rosario all dressed up. I go to her and brush against her legs while I meow, she picks me up, hugs me tightly and gives me a kiss which I feel has left a red mark on my head like on other occasions... I´ll just go to Adela to wipe it away for me when she leaves. She asks Marcos to call Juan.

"Please get the car ready, I'm going back to work today. I just need to make a call and I'll be out in five minutes."

Juan nods and leaves while I immediately go into panic mode when I hear her words. Is she going where she says she is? Is there a possibility she can somehow see Javier outside the house? If that is the case, how can we protect her?

FIFTEEN

ROSARIO

I read disappointment and anger in the face of my staff when they learn of my decision of not leaving Javier and letting him stay on in the pool house. I know they can't see past what happened, when someone does something really horrible, we find it so difficult to see beyond that, we just seem to focus only on the act they commit and can't find anything good in that person and I really don't blame them. I can't remember anything good about my husband either, everything he has ever done just seems like part of a project that only he is privy to.

When Javier asked to speak to me, I had everything so clear in my mind. The week I had spent in bed had given me time to look at what I had become; a shadow of my former self, better said, "A scared shadow of my former self". So while I waited for the external injuries and bruises to heal, I decided to address my internal wounds, or at least try. I have always stood tall and proud, never letting anyone make me feel small and insignificant; that is what my parents instilled in me as soon as I was able to understand words, they made each and every one of their children look at themselves and know that they could take on the world and whatever it threw at them, we had it in us, we were good enough for any and every situation. I have spent so much time hiding from the world, trying to cement over every single crack that appeared in my carefully constructed life, a life that was a lie; I have lost myself in the process along with the will to live. All this because I gave someone the power to humiliate me and make me feel smaller and smaller every day. I decided after so many years of being constantly humiliated that I needed to look into that same mirror that I grew up with, that mirror that made me feel like I was Rosario Domínguez González again.

I said I would listen to him because I wanted to get it over and done with as soon as possible. I wanted to close the chapter of my life that had only brought me pain in every sense of the word. I would tell my parents that things had not worked out; I still could not admit the truth to anyone that had not seen what had taken place, least of all my parents! They would be heartbroken and there was no need for anyone else to feel my pain. I know they would be disappointed in me because they wouldn't understand or accept my decision but if I let that man kill me, somehow that would kill them too.

As I listen to Javier and hear him open up to me in a way that he had never done before, I feel my resolve weakening. Hearing his voice break and seeing his hands shake as he tries to put into words some form of explanation for the last five years of our lives, makes an emotion that has always been within me rise to the surface, it is guilt.

I find myself feeling guilty for wanting to walk away and leave the horror behind because I know that somehow one day, I will be free of it and I will be able to escape but he will always have to live with what he has done; he can't run away from himself. So, when he asks me for more time because he needs help, I feel that I can't in good conscience deny him that. There are things my mother told me when I was young that have never left me. I imagined her saying something I had heard her say on many occasions to my father, my brothers and I... "Was that your best?"

If I left now, my answer would be, no. Through the years, his violence has escalated to a point where hitting me seems like a natural reflex action to him. He had never spoken of getting help before because he probably didn't think he needed any, if I go he would not have any reason for wanting to change and I would somehow be responsible for the harm he would inflict on someone else as I suspect that he has become accustomed to what he does and he can no longer control himself. I find myself saying that he can stay in the pool house, that he can't come into the main house and that when he is better, I will leave him because I don't know how our marriage can recover from this.

"Let's not talk about our marriage at this point, I can't deal with that now, I just really need to find my way back to what I was before I turned into one of the worst villains I have ever seen both on and off-screen. I'm going to therapy and anger management; my 'shrink' would like to see you in the near future and also arrange a session at which we are both present. Do you think you would be willing to do that?

I have always been wary of such sessions as I feel people just go there to sit down, say what they want and pay for that... But the name Javier mentions is extremely well known and respected as a professional and I would like to know the opinion of someone who has probably dealt with a lot of similar cases, so I accept to do that later on.

Two weeks have passed since then; Javier has kept his word and hasn't come near me. I have hired two security guards, one for the day and one for the night. I never ever want to feel such fear and impotence again, the kind that starts from the pit of your stomach and makes you need to sit down because your legs can't support you. I also see that the staff check on me constantly and Balou seems to have taken his duties as my guardian to heart. He is practically the only thing that brings a smile to my face, I have seen him circle the pool house and somehow I know he is doing it for me. I feel incredibly lucky to have such a small and strong-willed companion by my side.

Finally, after the bruises have gone through all the colours and phases and I no longer feel a horrible pain when I move, I decide to go back to work as I need to make an effort to bring some normality back into my life; staying at home and breathing a sigh of relief each time I hear Javier's car leave the premises is driving me crazy. Also, I don't want to see something that is so important to me suffer because of my personal circumstances, people depend on me both to keep their jobs and also to make our projects happen. I am good at what I do. I'm not going to allow myself to lose that too.

Everyone is happy to see me; Pilar's mother is still in the hospital, which is a constant worry for her. I feel a sort of connection with her family because they somehow remind me of my own; they are a very close knit clan too. When I moved from Sevilla to Madrid after my marriage, I noticed that there was a different vibe in this city. In Sevilla you breathe tradition and if possible to imagine, even taste it. The family, both immediate and extended plays a very big part in our lives. In Madrid, I have felt that people just do their own thing and family ties are not as strong. Maybe it's because of my particular circumstances which have closed my mind from seeing anything good in my adopted city, but I miss people gathering in the house of one relation or the other without needing an invitation, to eat and talk at the top of their voices while one dish after the other are placed on the table. We have two houses, a *Cortijo*[7] in which we spend our holidays and some weekends and a typical manor house in the city, that surrounds an inner patio decorated with flowers and the special tiles you can find only in this part of the country, both of our residences always have people constantly coming and going, our table is always complete. When it's not too hot, you can always find a group of people sitting on the patio drinking *Fino* or *Manzanilla*[8] and eating

---

[7] A sort of big farmhouse. Normally located in rural areas and very popular in the south of Spain. It usually comprises of the main house that is surrounded by large extension of land, usually used for agricultural purposes.

[8] Very popular wines consumed in both the households and fairs of Sevilla made from the white grape originally from Jerez. They are often confused as the same thing but depending on how the wine is elaborated, you get either Fino or Manzanilla.

Pescaito frito[9]. Sometimes when I close my eyes, my mind returns to such happy memories and it is one of my safe places when things get really bad. I can count the times I have seen my mother-in-law since I moved here with the fingers of one hand and I'd still have fingers left. When we've gone to family celebrations with them, it's just different. Don't get me wrong, people laugh, are happy and have fun but I miss the sparkle of my people, their jokes, their accent... Pilar and her family remind me of that, so I hope her mother gets better soon as I know that their home seems lost and empty without her.

They bring me up to speed and I soon enter into the routine of work, there is a lot to be done. It is what I need to get my mind off the sorry state of my personal life.

Ever since Concha came to the house and I found out that she was not a completely innocent bystander to my predicament, I have wanted to confront her without the disadvantage of lying helpless on a bed. So the next day I ask Juan to take me to her house before going to work, I know that she has a class with her personal trainer every morning at eleven so I decide to get there for twelve and catch her before she goes off to one of her many lunches or meetings as she belongs to a ridiculous number of committees.

---

[9] A selection of different types of both fried fish and sea food.

Her house is located in one of the most exclusive areas of Madrid and just like mine, it was designed by her husband, it is a very grand mansion and as I sit in one of the three sitting rooms they have, the same thought of every single time I visit them comes to my mind, they have way too much furniture and ornamentation in the rooms. Concha collects antiques; actually she collects everything with an expensive price tag attached. So, the walls have too many paintings, the floors too many Persian carpets and there are too many vases from various Chinese Dynasties. I sometimes suspect that she has been sold some that are not authentic, but she shows them off with such great pride that I decide not to investigate further, even though a few times when she is not looking I look under the vases to see if I can get more information and search online for their authenticity. She can't have so many original items. My thoughts are interrupted as she walks into the room, as always she looks perfect, make up in place and she is wearing a suit that must be a Valentino who is her favourite designer.

As I stand up when she comes in, I think that I have nothing to be envious about as from the looks I have got I know I look stunning. I want to change the memory she has of the last time she saw me, so I have made sure that that my appearance today is impressive. I don't move towards her to give her the accustomed two kisses and I notice that she doesn't make any attempt to do so either.

"I was not expecting you. Rosario, you should have called first."

"I didn't want to give you the opportunity to make up an excuse not to see me, so I decided to just come. Besides, in all the time I have been married to your son, you have never once called before visiting, I'm extending you the same courtesy."

"Why would I not want to see you? Don't be silly, you people from the south are so dramatic[10]."

I look at her in amazement as she says this and I understand that she has had a lot of time to come up with a strategy of how to deal with what happened. She is a lioness protecting her cub and her claws are out.

"Really? Dramatic? Why don't I send these photographs to the press? Let's see what they have to say, they are quite self explanatory, nothing exaggerated in them."

I throw the photographs on the table near her and she comes closer to look at them. Adela and Marcos took them when I had refused to go to the hospital because she

---

[10] It is popularly said that people from Andalucía tend to exaggerate when relating events.

said I might need them one day and it was better to have them and not need them than the alternative.

"You took photographs of yourself in this state? With what purpose in mind? Do you want to blackmail us?"

"What could you possibly have that I'd want? Money, status... What? You can't give me anything because the only thing I want is to go back in time and have the good sense to say no to your son when he proposed, can you give me that?, I came here to get some sort of explanation from you, to ask why you sat down so comfortably in the front row of my wedding, knowing you were condemning me to this life."

"These photographs don't mean anything, if you show them to anyone you would need to prove that my son did that to you and the night you were beaten up, he was having dinner here with me. He is a very intelligent young man but to this date, he still does not possess the ability to be in two places at the same time. You must have angered one of your many lovers and he took things too far."

I stare at her in disbelief with my mouth open, now I have lovers? Wondering if she has convinced herself of her version, she returns my stare and I laugh out loud, it just seems so surreal, it's like watching a bad television movie, except this is my life and that thought suddenly sobers me up.

"Four people saw him do that, this time he didn't even wait to make sure no one could see him, he didn't care. So there are people who can come out and destroy the alibi you have so carefully constructed."

"Which people?"

"Our staff, they all saw it."

"Well considering you pay their salaries, they will say anything you want them to. I will discredit each and every one of them in a court of law."

"A court of law? By the time I send out these photographs to all the reputable magazines, TV stations and newspapers in the country, I can assure you that the public opinion will judge and condemn him. I have reporters that are constantly asking me for interviews and quotes, I will not lack platforms to explain everything. But you know what? I'm not going to play this game with you, I am going to proceed to send them out and let's see who wins this war."

I start gathering them and when I look up, I read fear in her eyes. I turn to walk towards the door.

"Please don't do that, you will destroy my family."

"Why should I do anything for you? You let me marry your son. You should not have let him marry anyone at all to

~ 128 ~

begin with, he is not fit to be in a relationship, he is unable to love and now that your worst suspicions have come true, you prefer sweeping everything under the carpet and denying it all. You have even put the blame on an invented lover of mine. You have given me no reason to feel pity for you or your own."

As I shout out these words, she sits down, covers her face with her hands and starts crying and I'm frankly too angry to care, her tears mean absolutely nothing to me, I can't bring out any compassion in me for that woman when she has shown none for me.

"You were supposed to be like a mother to me, protect me and take care of me but instead you let your son destroy me day after day and put my life in danger. Do you know what it is to lie awake at night and fear for my life? Do you? How can you still defend him? How can you not want him to be locked away somewhere where he can no longer harm anyone?"

"You don't understand, you don't have children so you don't know what it is to want to protect someone with your life. I have not been able to sleep since I found out what happened, I was horrified when I walked into that room and saw the state you were in, I haven't told my husband because he was extremely angry when he hit the other girl. He made it clear then that he wouldn't tolerate anything similar. He wanted to call the police then, I was the one who begged him to pay her off but if he learns about this..."

"He didn't just hit her, he left her unconscious for you to find, not caring whether she was alive or not, stop removing importance from everything your son does. If he hasn't killed anyone yet, it is because he has been lucky. But if something is not done he will do so soon and your husband's anger will be the least of your worries. Who is the girl in question?"

"Someone he dated, it was some time ago."

"Who was she?"

"She was a beauty-queen from one of the states, nobody important."

I look at her as she says this and I see that for her the only important thing is her beloved son, in order to accept the kind of person he is, she puts the blame on everybody else. I'm sure the other girl was wayward and a gold-digger, she has convinced herself of this too. I store the little information she has given me about the girl and decide to do my own research.

"What are you going to do? Please no one can find out, he has told me that he is getting help and that this time, it's different. He is really sorry for what he did. When he confessed it all to me, I saw that it was destroying him."

"What does his being sorry do for me? I can´t stay married to someone that has done that to me. As soon as he has recovered, I will leave him. Don´t worry, for the sake of my family I will not bring out all the ugly details of my marriage that you are so afraid of, I do know what it is to love people beyond myself and I too will do anything to protect them from my pain, the only difference between you and me is that, you are protecting a potential killer."

"Oh and by the way, you should put that animal to sleep. He is dangerous, look at what he did to Javier´s face; he had to receive medical treatment to prevent the wounds from getting infected."

I feel the anger rise in me and I´m about to answer her and say things I would probably deeply regret later but instead I pick up two of her most expensive looking vases and I smash them against the wall and this makes me feel much better than if I had shouted or insulted her. She screams and kneels down to pick up the pieces, while one of her maids rushes in to see what has happened.

I walk out of the house with her sobs still ringing in my ears. No matter what I do, I´m going to hurt someone. I just have to decide who deserves it more.

SIXTEEN

BALOU

The days turn into weeks and little by little some form of normality is restored to the household. It does help that "Cold Eyes" is actually keeping his promise and staying out of our way. I have crossed paths with him a few times in the drive way or when I have gone to make my rounds. We have stared at each other and it is clear that we both feel something akin to hatred but he is very careful and has not tried to touch me or hit me, even when no one is looking. I heard Rosario tell Adela that he was getting help for his problem and had I been able to contribute to the conversation, I would have told them that there was no possible change or redemption for that man, he likes what he is and the power he has over people when they are afraid of him. He is a predator; I am one so I know what it feels like, the surge of adrenaline that the hunt and kill brings is addictive.

At the end of the day, her inability to accept what he is, is putting her life in danger and this complicates things for those around her. Especially for me, I'm a strong believer in "the law of minimum effort" and so far I'm not getting too many opportunities to be true to it; my loyalty requires me to stay alert and on my toes. I do make sure I get my required fourteen hours of sleep during the day though.

Rosario goes out to work every day, at least she is not spending her days looking at a fixed spot on the wall, but I see no joy in her eyes and she hardly sleeps at night. She tosses and turns a lot and sometimes I hear her mumble in her sleep or wake up suddenly, shaking. I also see her look through the windows at the pool house. I guess she is also nervous about having him around. Still I do my bit and keep her busy. She always spends close to an hour playing with me when she gets back from work and my favourite game is "Catch me if you can". I run up to her, tap her ankle and then run away so she has to chase me, then when she turns around after catching up with me, I'll repeat the process. I also like hide and seek and jumping out from behind the doors.

Since she orders my food, I always wait anxiously for the delivery man to arrive once a month with the huge boxes. I normally sit on them until she comes home so everyone knows that they are mine and also so we can open them together. When this happens, I proceed to inspect the contents of the boxes while she brings out one item after the other. There was always a new toy and a lot of treats. I have nothing but respect for a woman who is not afraid to use her credit card generously.

One day, I hear her say that with everything that had happened she had not had time to take me to the vet to have me neutered. I have no idea what neutered means but the word "vet" is one I am very familiar with and it never ends well for me. Apart from the fact that he keeps complaining about my weight, ignorant man, he has still not learnt that I´m a perfect specimen of my breed. He prods me, opens my mouth in a very inelegant way, injects me... So this can´t be good.

I see my carrier is in the hall way, she always leaves it there prior to a trip to that horrible place. I don´t know why she does that, I actually prefer the element of surprise, knowing what is in store for me, just makes me nervous. That night, I´m not given any food... I think they must have forgotten so I go to Adela and meow and meow but she only pats my head and says she can´t give me anything. Can´t? I find her words extremely confusing. As soon as Rosario comes in I am very vocal in my complaint that I haven't been fed, thinking she would wrong the right immediately, but instead she scoops me up and takes me to her room. So for the first time in my life, for a strange reason, I am not given my supper and I go to bed hungry. I am extremely confused, is she trying to implement some form of diet? If this is the case, I will not stand for it. I can't have spent so much time training them about my feeding habits for this to happen now.

To my great surprise, I don't get any breakfast the next day either; is the plan to starve me to death? But before I can make my feelings appropriately known... Juan unceremoniously puts me into the carrier and I'm taken to the car. I look through the side slits and I see Adela has come to the car and is making soothing noises; this can't bode well, so I meow until we get there and as usual this results in me losing my voice.

I hate the waiting room; people bring in other animals, a lot of owners don't hold their dogs and they come over to smell and sniff my carrier, barking in the process, something I find most annoying. If we were out in the street, things would be different. I also hate the smell the place has; it is very strong and unpleasant.

We wait for a few minutes, Rosario speaks to me through the hole in my carrier while I push myself as far as possible from the door, the moment she opens it my pupils are already dilated from sheer panic. Then the horrible vet comes out and calls my name, he normally calls out the name of the pet instead of the owner, I don't know if he thinks that knowing my name wins him any points with me... I can assure you, it does not help at all.

He hands me over to his nurse while he tells Rosario that she can't stay. When I hear this I get even more scared, what is he going to do to me that she can't watch? She has always been by my side. The last image I have of her as I'm taken into an inner room is that she is wringing her hands and asking about the risks of the procedure. Risks?

I have to be encouraged to get out of the carrier as I decide that I will not willingly come out of it or help them in any way. Suddenly, I am injected with something and I find that I can't keep my eyes open. I wake up and it feels like no time has passed at all. I find it difficult to fix my gaze on anything and I don't know where I am, I try to stand up and just fall back down. I seem to be in some type of cage. I try to meow but no sound comes out. The nurse comes near my cage and looks at me while she writes down something in an open folder.

"Good, you are awake."

From her words, it seems I fell asleep. She brings my carrier and carefully places me inside. I feel sore for some reason but I have absolutely no idea why. She takes me to the examining room and Rosario is there, she jumps out of her seat as soon as I'm brought in. She takes the carrier from the nurse, she looks at me and I read anxiety in her eyes. What has she let them do to me?

"Are you sure he is fine? He seems disoriented. I have read that some cats don't respond well to anesthesia and have really bad reactions."

"He is perfect; he will be running around the house like nothing has happened before you know it."

When we get home, everyone is there to see me come out of the carrier, I find it difficult to maintain my balance or even walk in a straight line. I look at Rosario, she is following me as I try to get away from her, I hope she can read in my eyes, that if she has taken something from me that is important, I will have to add her to my list of the unloved and unwanted in my life.

SEVENTEEN

ROSARIO

    I haven't been able to follow-up on Javier's first recorded victim as I have been preoccupied with Balou's neutering. Because of everything that had happened I left it a few months later than I had wanted. I did a lot of research which led me to believe it is a fairly simple procedure for male cats and the chances of something going wrong are very slim. But I worry that he would be in the small percentage of cats that don't tolerate anesthesia. Still, I know it's what is best for him, but I also know that not feeding him eight hours before the procedure will be torture. Balou does not allow us to mess with his feeding times, nothing distracts him. Sure enough he is very vocal about the fact that he hasn't been fed and it is really difficult hearing him meow and not be able to give him anything. I try to comfort him while we are in the waiting room, I notice his pupils are dilated as he looks at me and meows in such a pitiful way, I'm tempted to take him away and forget about it, but we have come so far and I don't want to go through the experience of not feeding him for another night.

The vet does not allow me go in with him; they say they will call me as soon as he was awake so I can collect him. I spend the hours looking and reading about similar cases online and checking my phone to see if they have called me incase something has gone wrong. If Balou dies, I don't know what I'd do, he is the reason why I feel like waking up every day. I know I have a lot of others reasons to do so but at the moment, he is the only thing that keeps me going. I call the vets practice a few times but I can't learn anything new from the reception desk, I don't care if the veterinary nurse thinks I'm tiresome, she won't mourn for him if things go horribly wrong. I don't know if this is good or bad that she has no information for me.

Finally at four o'clock I get the call that I can pick him up and that everything went well, I rush out of the house and call Juan to take me to collect him. When we get back, he is let out of the carrier; he looks at me with reproach and keeps trying to get away from me. It's like he knows something has been done to him. He goes to hide under the bed, he hid there the day Javier beat me up. I know it is his safe place. Adela and I put out various plates to tempt him, but he stays put, so I decide to sleep in that room with him. In the middle of the night I'm woken to the sound of Balou munching, I smile as I know that is a good sign.

He is a bit quieter the next day... but, two days after, I hear him running up and down the stairs, I know that he is going to be just fine.

I spend the day after his operation at home so I can monitor him and see if there are any side effects, I don't want to miss a thing. Cats are well known for hiding pain and sometimes it is too late when their owners see the signs that something is wrong. This gives me time to research Javier's love life prior to the unfortunate day I met him.

The good thing about being public personalities in the age of the internet is that you can find anything about someone's past online. I knew he'd had a number of girlfriends before, I had seen him on the cover of magazines with different women, but I had never looked them up on the internet before. I have never liked knowing about the romantic history of the person I'm with, except in this instance, I felt something abnormal had happened, now I wish I had taken more of an interest... but, then I wouldn't have found out anything as they made sure what occurred didn't become public knowledge. I go to the search site and I'm surprised, there is quite an impressive list of women he has dated. I start looking for a beauty queen and I find that he dated Miss Valencia. I find various articles about them and it says they dated for a few months; they seemed to go everywhere together. I find various articles and photographs, in which she is gazing adorably at him and then all of a sudden she had made a written statement saying they had broken up. I look for more about them, but there is no mention of the reason for their split anywhere. I try to find out what became of her, but it seemed that after their separation she disappeared from the limelight. I spend a few minutes looking at her photographs; she was a tall, blonde and beautiful woman. I call my office and ask Pilar to get me her address and telephone number.

Half an hour later, the ever efficient Pilar sends me the information.

I telephone her and it goes to voice mail so I leave a message for her to please return my call. I'm surprised to find that she lives in Madrid, it is a small world.

That evening I get a call from her; I ask her if she can meet me for a drink the next day. She doesn't ask me what I want and agrees to meet me in a well known bar at eleven in the morning.

I arrive at the agreed venue and take a good look around, I can´t see anyone that fits her description, or anyone that looks like her various photographs I have seen online. I then notice a hand waving at me, as I approach the table I find it difficult to connect the person I´m looking at with the girl I saw online the previous day. She has put on so much weight, but her eyes are the same deep blue. I hold out my hand and she takes it in hers...

"Eva? Thanks for meeting me."

The waiter comes over and I ask her what she wants, we both order coffees and she asks for some toast as well. I look at her, I have no idea what pushed me to meet this woman, but now that I have her in front of me, I don´t know what I want to say or where to begin. I feel I´m intruding in something that must be extremely personal for her but as we are both here, I finally pluck up the courage to say something...

"You must be wondering why I asked to meet you..."

"I´m guessing it has to do with what happened between Javier and I. It is the only reason that I can think of, if you are worried that I´m going to say anything, I won´t. I´ve kept my promise and have not spoken to anyone about it."

"I'm sorry to bring it up, I really don't know what I expected but I just found out recently about what happened and I really need to hear it from you and try to understand what occurred."

"I never in my wildest dreams imagined I'd be having this conversation with you. I saw your wedding and from time to time I read about you. I also see that you are involved an abused women Foundation so I guess some of your interest comes from there."

I nod as I can't trust myself to speak whilst she butters her toast and takes a small bite from it. She has a distant look as she begins to relate her story.

"I have not spoken about this to anyone but the memories are so vivid, it's as if it happened yesterday. I had won the Miss Valencia pageant and I had gone on to represent my state in the Miss Spain competition. I finished second runner up and also won Miss Photogenic. This was very good for me as it encouraged model agencies to set their sights on me and offer me contracts; sometimes the runners-up get work more than the actual winners. I moved to Madrid where everything was happening, a few of us did that, some have even ended up working in television. I see them from time to time on different programmes. I got contracts with a few fashion designers and also for publicity campaigns, things were going well and I was being noticed. It was a world I was passionate about and in which I wanted to make a name for myself."

"One night a few of us went to a night club, one of the girls I shared an apartment with had been invited by a wealthy business man who was interested in her, she didn´t want to go alone, so she asked us to go with her. It was a very exclusive place, entry strictly by invitation. We had just got to Madrid and we loved going to new places and making new contacts. Javier walked in with a few friends, I looked at him and from that moment I was hooked, we were a group of good-looking girls, so they came over, he must have seen something he liked because he bought me a drink and asked for my number."

"The next day he called me and asked me to dinner and before long we were inseparable. He was so attentive, he would send me flowers, take me out, he was everything I wanted. I fell in love with him, who wouldn´t?"

"I started getting more calls... people wanted the face of Javier Cantora´s girlfriend linked to their brands. I signed a lot of contracts and I was happy because for me it was something real, I thought he felt the same way about me. Then one weekend he invited me to a house they have in the country, he was more quiet than usual but when I asked he said there was nothing wrong. So I let it be, he was working and studying at the same time so I knew he was under a lot of pressure. To this day I have no idea what set him off. I remember I asked if I could change the TV channel as he was reading the paper; as he didn´t answer, I went ahead and did just that. He lowered the paper and yanked the remote control from my hands, I was shocked as I had never seen him react in such a way before, I asked what was wrong and that is when he flipped. He just started shouting abuse at me and hitting me, I tried to defend myself but the blows just kept coming in. I woke up to his parents and a doctor watching over me, Javier was nowhere in sight. He had split my lip and broken three of my ribs..."

I listen to a story that is so familiar to me and I see that there are tears in her eyes and it dawns on me that she has not moved on, she has not been able to forget what had happened. On the other hand, why should she? Why should she have got over it? I suddenly feel annoyed for her that Javier just walked away and continued living his life, whilst time has stood still for her.

"I came here today to see if you had answers for me. His parents gave me a cheque for an incredible amount of money, it was a life-changing figure, they also gave me a confidentiality agreement to sign... I´m breaking that by speaking to you, but I had to risk it, I just need to know why he did that to me. I never saw or spoke to him again. Did I do something wrong'? What happened?"

"I wish I had answers for you but I´m at a loss too. I have no idea why he did what he did. Like I said I´m just finding out now and I thought you could clarify it for me. Was he on drugs?"

"If he was I never saw him take any."

"What have you done in all these years with yourself? Did you get help?"

"I fell apart, I couldn´t come to terms with what happened, my work suffered, less and less people called me and I started stress eating, which is why you looked right at me when you came in without recognising me. I hardly go out now, I did go to therapy for a while but it really didn´t help me to stop wallowing in self pity. I see him on television and he is even better looking now, sometimes I wonder if I hadn't dreamt it all. I´m sorry, I shouldn´t have said the good looking part."

"It is fine. I´m sorry this happened, I wish I could offer you an explanation or give you some form of closure, you deserve it and somehow giving you money can´t possibly have made up for what happened. How could they have done that?"

"He was their son, they had to protect him. I think most parents would have done the same. Also they are very well known, a scandal like that would brand them for life. At the time I took the money and signed the contract I wasn't thinking straight. I just wanted to disappear and lick my wounds in private."

"You are young, you have your whole life ahead of you, don't let this be the only constant memory you have. Don't give it any more power over you. Please do something with your life."

I listen to the words that I find so apt for her and wonder why I'm finding it so difficult to think the same myself. I look at her and behind all that fat, she is still an incredibly attractive woman. I offer her my card and ask her to please contact me at the Foundation so I can find a way to help her. As I leave her, I come to terms with the fact that what has scared me most is the fact that I read in her eyes that she is still in love with Javier.

EIGHTEEN

BALOU

As the weeks go by, we settle into some sort of routine. I keep an eye open for warning signs of possible threats to her safety, but I have to say, I can´t find anything that screams out "Danger". I keep up my daily patrols, I don´t want to miss the writing on the wall. The staff are also very watchful and I have to say that having the security men around has really eased the tension for everyone.

Rosario seems more relaxed, she goes to work every day and I think this is good for her; as Javier is also out all day, I get time to do what we cats enjoy doing most, eat, sleep, rest, eat…

I have no idea who cooks for Javier now that he doesn't come into the house and I know Adela does not do it for him. In all the time Rosario and Javier lived together I didn't see him go into the kitchen once but I did see him eat a lot. But, it really doesn't bother me that he has lost his feeding privileges. The pool house has a big glass sliding door and when I make my daily inspection of the area, I try to peer through when the curtains are drawn but I can't see much. From time to time, a young girl is brought in a car to clean his living quarters.

He leaves and comes back at different times to Rosario, so they don't really see each other, which is perfect. Would I be happier if we never saw him again? Of course, but if my hearing did not fail me when they spoke, she told him she would stay with him until he got better, then she would leave. I understand that she will take me with her as the idea of remaining behind has never crossed my mind. Where would we go? I do wonder... I look into his eyes when we cross paths to see if I can tell if he has changed for the better, but I don't see anything, only emptiness.

So you can imagine my great shock when one sunny morning just as Rosario is getting into her car, he calls out to her. I'm happily munching on a piece of grass when this happens, I feel my heart literally skip a beat and I run towards her. Juan is standing nearby, he was about to drive her somewhere and I see that he has tensed up. I missed the first part of the conversation but then you don´t have to be a genius to know what he wants.

"I have been going to see the psychologist every day, he says I´m making very good progress, he would like for you to come in at some point, whenever you are ready, no pressure. But it is important for him to hear your side of the story so he can access the situation properly. He says a lot of people delude themselves and create an alternate reality, he needs to know and see the extent of the harm I did."

"I don´t know if..."

"Just think about it please. I really need you to understand what goes through my mind and that you are the most important thing to me, I can´t believe how toxic and destructive I have become."

He touches her arm and walks away, I look at her while I panic, hoping that she does not believe anything he says. It is another of his games, I mean; surely she must see that as clearly as I do. But as I stare at her, I see that the look of sadness that she had some time ago, was back. She gets into the car and Juan drives her away.

Later that evening, when our little vigilante group is in the kitchen; Juan relates what happened that morning to them all. I can tell by their reactions that the news has upset them.

"He is going to suck her in again, into the darkness he kept her in for a long time. Such people don't change, why didn't he get help before? Now that he is in danger of being exposed, he says he is on the road to recovery. I don't believe it", says Adela, shaking her head while she unloads the dishwasher.

"Did she say anything in the car?" asks Marcos.

"She was very quiet, from time to time I glanced at her through the rear view mirror and she seemed very far away. I have no idea what is going to happen but I fear that soon, that man will return to this house. I know people deserve second chances but I just don't know..."

I knew! I knew that that man had not changed, why did they still have doubts? They all agree to keep a more vigilant eye on him. All this makes me restless again, waiting for something to happen and not knowing when or what.

Two days later, I see Rosario leave the house through the back so I follow her and to my horror, she walks in the direction of the pool house.

NINETEEN

ROSARIO

I wake up suddenly at three in the morning, I hear a strange noise, it takes me a second to realise that it´s the telephone ringing. I pick up and can´t understand what is being said on the other end of the line as a woman is crying and talking at the same time. I´m now fully awake and it takes two attempts of me asking what is going on before I finally realise that it is Pilar trying to tell me her mother just died.

I jump out of bed and get dressed quickly, she tells me the body has been taken to the *Tantorio M30*[11] for the

---

[11] M30 morgue in Madrid.

wake. As I rush out of the house, I bump into Javier in the drive way.

"Hey are you okay?"

"Yes I'm fine. I got a call from Pilar, her mother just died and I'm on my way to be with her."

"I am sorry to hear that. Let me take you in my car."

"No it's fine. I can manage."

"Really? Your hands are shaking, it's 3 am and you don't like driving at night."

Javier takes the keys from me, leaving me no room for further argument. We get into the car and he drives us there in complete silence. Ever since he asked me to attend a session with his therapist, I have been making an extra effort to avoid him as it's not something I'm particularly looking forward to.

My thoughts turn to Pilar and her family. I remember the first time I saw her.

My mother has a very special interest in the Foundation, when I moved to Madrid and we opened the branch here, she spent a week with me to help out. Up till then, we had operated from Sevilla, two of my cousins ran it and my mother and aunts were very involved, so we decided they would concentrate in the national projects and the Madrid branch would operate in other countries.

On the day we were holding interviews to hire the staff; my mother was with me in the conference hall. We had seen five people for the post of my assistant, they were all graduates and two of them had a post graduate degree and then Pilar came in. She didn´t have any previous experience and this put me off as I wanted someone that would just hit the ground running and not need to be taught practically everything. Two more candidates came in and after they had all gone, we both discussed all the applicants and their resumés. I had liked a young man that had spent some time working for an NGO in Kenya, he spoke with confidence and talked us through setting up projects, but my mother had other ideas.

"I liked the girl with the finger Rosary."

"Who?"

"The plump girl in the blue dress."

"Mama, you can´t pick a candidate for a job just because she is wearing a religious symbol."

My mother is a devout catholic and she gives a lot of importance to her faith, so for her, the ring Pilar wore was a sign that we had to hire her.

"I'm telling you that girl is perfect for the post."

"She is the least qualified, I'm not even going to consider her. She would only give the others more work. I need someone who will do things even without being asked. Sometimes the church going people are the worst ones, I can't use that as a parameter to give someone a job."

My mother looked at me for a few seconds, she shook her head while she put Pilar's folder on the top of the pile.

"Well just imagine how they would be if they didn't believe in God."

With those words, she ended the conversation and of course I gave her the post because even though we have different methods of doing things, to this day, my mother has always been right when it comes to sizing people up.

On the first day of work, Pilar came in with a homemade cheesecake from her mum; it was to thank me for giving her the opportunity. Later she told me that she initially hadn't intended applying for the job as when she read the requisites she saw that she wasn't qualified for it but her mother encouraged her and they both prayed that she would get it. When I told my mother this, she looked at me and nodded in satisfaction. I have to say that what she lacked in experience she made up for with the enthusiasm she put into everything she did and before long I came to depend on her to keep on top of everything. I met her mother on two occasions and it was really touching to see the way she cared for her family, it was like having my mother in front of me, I couldn´t even begin to imagine what they were all going through.

I noticed the car was slowing down as we entered the parking lot, soon we found the room where her family and friends are watching over her for the last time. There are a lot of people there, I spot Pilar sitting amongst some other women, the one next to her is patting her knee and talking to her, she raises her head and sees me so she gets up and comes towards me. We embrace and at that moment, words fail me. There is nothing I can say that can possibly comfort her, she says hello to Javier and I notice that her eyes are red and puffy. I go with her into the inner chamber to see the open coffin and say my last adieu. There is a priest praying and some people that must be members of her family standing next to the body with their heads bowed. We spend an hour with them during which time a lot of people come and go. We leave to get some rest as the funeral is at 10.00 am, later that morning.

Javier excuses himself as he can´t attend and this is frankly a relief for me. I want to be able to be there for Pilar without the extra tension of having him by my side. When I go into the church I see that the family are sitting at the front and that people are going up to them to offer their condolences before the mass starts. I spot my staff and I go and sit next to them, they have all come to support their colleague, everyone at the office likes Pilar, she is a ray of sunshine to us all.

I haven´t been in a church in some time but when the mass begins a lot of memories start coming back to me. Sevilla is full of religious tradition, the processions at Easter are spectacular, people come from different parts of the world just to see them and a lot of us grew up in families that partake in these events with a passion.

Mine is one such family, when we were young we were all part of the confraternity of *"Nuestro Padre Jesús del Gran Poder"*;[12] every year we would be dressed in black robes and hoods and accompany the statue being carried in procession through the streets of Sevilla to the Cathedral, while the band played and from time to time someone would

---

[12] Translation: Our Father Jesus of the great power.

burst into a spontaneous *Saeta*[13]. For me it was a way of life, a part I would walk away from in time but for my mother, it was her life and not just something she did once a year for the benefit of others. She still takes part in the procession every year and we watch her from the crowd or if we get there on time, from a nearby balcony close to where the procession is passing.

When we were young, we would all go to mass as a family on Sundays. For all of us except my mother, it was just something we did, I doubt we really understood what was taking place, I know I didn´t. When I was seventeen I started going out to pubs and staying out late with my friends, I would wake up late on Sunday and I so I wasn´t ready on time to go with them. Little by little I stopped going, it was the same with most of my friends as we would also go out on Sunday in the evenings, so we really didn´t find the appropriate time to go to church. This deeply saddened my mother as she went to mass daily, I caught her looking at me a few times with an expression I couldn´t read but

---

[13] This is a traditional religious song normally performed in the processions of The Holy Week in Spain; this is very popular in Andalucia. Nowadays, they are mostly saetas usually sung in the flamenco style of music as a sign of devotion from low balconies in houses as the images corresponding to the Easter period are carried through the streets. This is very representative of the art and tradition of the south of Spain.

somehow I felt it was connected to this. She did not force me to go or make me feel guilty for not doing so and as soon as Miguel and Soledad were of age, they followed in my footsteps. We did however go at Christmas, Easter and a few other important occasions.

For my father on the other hand it was a different matter, for him, it was just the right thing to do, it was also an opportunity to go for the traditional *Aperitivo*[14] after church with their friends to a bar or pub. But one day, it became clear to us that my mother was the only true believer in the family.

We had all gone to church as it was my mother's birthday and each year when we asked what she wanted us to get her, she would reply "to accompany her to mass on that day and pray for her." That day the church was full and there was nowhere to park. As we were now late and after circling the area a couple of times without any luck, my father left us at the door while he looked for a parking space. He assumed that everyone would leave after the mass so parked his car in such a way that he was blocking someone else's. However, this person left earlier than expected and called for the car

---

[14] This is a very popular practice in Spain, before lunch people go down to a bar or pub for a glass of wine/beer usually accompanied with a *tapa*. A very good excuse to meet up and chat with friends.

in question to be towed, when we came out a little later we saw that our means of transport had gone. My father was enraged and even though his car was quickly brought back, he got into an argument with Padre Alberto, this resulted in him announcing loudly in front of the crowd that had gathered around them to witness the spectacle that he "was never setting foot in the church again."

We went back home in silence, my father was furious and kept muttering under his breath, at that moment it became clear to me that his faith was as strong as mine.

About half an hour later, we all rushed into the kitchen, we were drawn there by the loud voices. My parents seldom quarreled, it was normal to hear my father shout as he had a fiery temper coupled with a good set of lungs, but not my mother, she hardly ever raised her voice, so when she did we knew it was for something serious. We all stood in the doorway looking from one to the other, it was quite scary. My father is very tall and strong and my mother is plump and petite, but she was just as angry as he was, looking up at him without faltering or wavering. As it was a Sunday, the staff were thankfully on their day off, so they didn´t see the uncomfortable scene.

"I have said I´m not going and that is final. How can you expect me to go back after the way that priest spoke to me?"

"How he spoke to you? You showed no respect whatsoever. He merely pointed out that your car was not properly parked. Was he the one that had your car towed?"

"You are the one that is not respecting me, you should have stood by me instead of apologising to your priest. Your loyalty is to me, I am your husband."

"You made me feel ashamed of being married to you today and I will not reward bad behaviour, neither in my children nor in my husband."

I looked at my younger brothers who were holding hands, they watched what was going on with their eyes wide open, I decided to take them away and just as I turned to do that, my father shouted "You have several drivers at your disposal, from now on they will take you"

"Miguel am I a widow?"

"Evidently not."

"Then hear me well, the day I sit alone in church, is the day that you are no longer in this world. You will not make me feel your absence before it´s time. So you can either sit by my side and pray to God to teach you about respect and forgiveness towards others or you can fall sleep for all I care but I will not go for Sunday mass alone."

We all held our breath and expected to hear the thunderous voice of my father, especially as my mother had uttered those last words in a very calm voice while she was chopping onions, but he just looked at her for a very long time, then turned around and stormed out of the room. The next Sunday, they both left the house together, the few times a year when we went with them, my brothers and I would nudge each other and look at my father who had an unmistakable look of resignation on his face.

Still there must have been a little faith in him because the one time my mother was absent from our home for a week because she was seriously ill with pneumonia in the hospital, my father left the house at the same time she used to every morning when she went for mass... when I asked him about it, he said that he felt he needed to be there, just in case someone was really listening. So the next day we all went with him, we felt there was strength in numbers.

I am brought back into the present as everyone turns to the next person to offer the sign of peace. There are tears in my eyes for the woman we are burying today and for all the memories that coming here have brought back to me because even if I had gone to church with my family grudgingly, it was a time when I had actually been really happy.

I have missed the sermon that the young priest has given as I have been absent with my thoughts the whole time but after we accompany Pilar and her family to lay to rest the remains of her mother, I find myself asking Padre Antonio if he can hear my confession.

TWENTY

BALOU

This is not the life I expected to have. Yes I am well fed, I am loved and I have the freedom to come and go as I please but I don´t have the rest and leisure time I would have wanted. I don´t want to spend my time worrying about anyone or wondering whenever next something horrible will happen. I´m supposed to eat, sleep, prey and hunt. That is my natural cycle, with a very long period of sleep, but this is something that has become a luxury for me.

I have become a silent part of the meetings in the kitchen with the four workers. Their conversations do not put my mind at ease as it is clear that they trust "Cold Eyes" as much as I do. Every day while Adela invites them to a coffee and cake or something else to eat, they each recount where they have seen Javier and they analyse the situation. This has brought them all much closer, when I first arrived there was a respectful distance between them all and they only entered cook's territory when they wanted something in particular. I have even lost my distrust for Marcos and Marylin as I have seen that we all share the same common goal, protecting Rosario. I wish I was human because if that had been the case, we would not be wasting so much time just talking. That man would be locked away somewhere without any hope of ever seeing daylight again. I get impatient because they are respecting Rosario's wishes, but sometimes one has to look at the greater good, especially when it is clear that she is not thinking straight.

The other night, I was sleeping by her side on her pillow; I practically jumped out of my skin when I was abruptly woken up by the sound of the telephone. She dressed quickly and rushed out the door as I ran behind her. I didn't see Javier either, until she ran right into him, but I felt fear when I saw her stop to talk to him, that feeling escalated when she got into the car with him. I waited outside until she returned and I was extremely vocal with my disapproval to her, she just picked me up and patted my head. I'm beginning to think that I am the most intelligent creature here. How on earth can she give that man even a second of her time?

--

Over the following days I intensify my watch and patrol the perimeter of the pool house. What is even more frustrating is that I´m alone in this, as it happened at night, none of the others were present to see this. Nobody will see it coming, except me and my abilities to help are limited.

When Rosario is home, I never leave her side, except to eat of course, I´m glad that my appetite is still a constant in my life, I´m not going to allow that man take that from me. So I am present when Rosario gets a call and accepts an invitation to meet someone in half an hour in the garden. I didn´t catch the name of the person she was talking to, but when it´s time, I bound outside with her and when I hear the approaching footsteps, I turn around and am horrified to see Javier walking towards us. I hiss and arch my back and he stops a few meters away from us, he doesn't take his eyes off me.

"It is evident that he does not like me."

"You threw him against the wall, animals have memories, especially when something bad happens, you could have killed him."

"I know and I´m really sorry. I can´t even remember half of what happened that day. Because I saw your bruises, I know it wasn´t a dream or a figment of my imagination.

"Javier, you keep referring to the last time you beat me up, the only thing different on that occasion was that the staff were there; but you have done this a number of times, each time taking it a step further. This was not a one off thing. You can´t excuse it in any way."

"I know, because you have told me, but if I have to be honest, I have absolutely no recollection of any other times. That is what scares me the most, I can´t seem to remember anything of that nature."

"Are you serious? There were times I stayed in my room for days because I couldn´t let anyone see the marks on my face, not even opening the door for Adela to bring in my food, she had to leave the tray outside the door for me to pick up after she had left."

I am listening intently to what is being said and I notice that Rosario has become quite agitated and is shouting at this point. Carlos who is responsible for the security at night comes out from his post at the gate when he hears the raised voices; he walks towards us and asks if everything is all right. I'm screaming inside "Of course it´s not, you idiot, Can´t you see?" But he is told everything is fine so he takes a walk around the house. I am torn between going with him and giving him an earful so he can feel my distress, but I decide to stay and protect Rosario and also find out why Javier asked to see her.

"I seem to have blackouts. When I started seeing the therapist and I relayed things to him, he advised me to have some tests done to see if there was a medical explanation for my behaviour, today I got the results... I have a brain lesion; the doctors think it might be related to the head injury I sustained eight years ago in the car accident. These are the results so you can see for yourself."

He hands her a file and Rosario sits down to read it, I notice her hands are trembling and she has difficulty turning the pages. Javier squats in front of her and touches her hand.

"I just want you to know that I would never, ever, deliberately hurt you; you have to believe me. I knew there had to be a reason and I am working very hard to see if I can make things right and ensure that this never happens again."

He turns around and leaves while I just sit back in amazement. I have to give it to him, the guy is a genius. He has found a logical explanation for his behaviour. I sense that Rosario is confused and the way she looks at him as he walks away seems different.

She spends the next few days glued to her computer, reading books and magazines, writing things down. I don´t know why the knowledge that Javier has a problem doesn´t make me feel any better or more importantly, safer.

TWENTY-ONE

ROSARIO

I'm standing next to Pilar when Padre Antonio comes over, he says some words of comfort to her and smiles as he passes me... I find myself asking him if he can hear my confession, he tells me that he has been called to administer the Sacrament to a dying man and that he had to rush to the hospital, but if I could stop by the parish later... I accept his offer, but I lose my nerve and go home without waiting for him.

I had remembered what it felt like telling someone things that you couldn't reveal to anyone else. Even though I no longer believed or practised my religion and I didn't know what I should be asking forgiveness for, there is something popularly known as "Catholic guilt". I needed the priest to tell me I was not doing anything wrong but most important was my mother's opinion of me; I wanted someone whose point of view she would respect to hear me out.

The days passed by and I kept putting it off but now I'm standing in front of the church; after Javier's revelation last night I just had to come here to clear my head.

I called and asked that he see me when he was free, I needed more than just five minutes of his time, we sit down in one of the back pews and I start talking. I had arrived very composed but I have to pause regularly because I can't stop crying. I tell him things I have never told anyone before or even dared say out loud, things that I have even hidden from this narrative because they are too personal to share with anyone else.

He listens to me without interrupting and I speak for over an hour, I show him the photographs that I carry everywhere with me in my bag of the last time he hit me. I know he must hear things like this all the time but this is my life and I really don't know how to come out of the darkness I find myself in without help, now it looks like he is my only option as I'm not ready to consider the other alternatives that I have.

"I used to think that I was a good person, I always tried to do things the best way I could but now I feel like I must have done something really horrible and I'm being punished for it. There really seems to be no other plausible explanation for what is happening to me."

"Things don't happen to people because they deserve them or not, people are not punished with, for example, cancer or the death of a loved one because of something they've done and I doubt that you are a bad person."

"I feel really terrible for wanting to leave and be as far away as I can from Javier, instead of staying by his side now that I have proof that he can't be held accountable for his actions. I have gone with him to various specialists who have explained everything to us and there is no doubt that he is telling the truth."

"I think the strange thing would have been for you to want to remain by his side after all that has happened."

I look up at Padre Antonio in surprise when he says this, I thought his first words would be to tell me about my duty and that I had to forgive him and stay with him as this was the "for better or worse and in sickness or in health" part of my vows.

"When Javier asked me to marry him, I went home and showed my mother my engagement ring, I was so happy and excited, she smiled and congratulated me without saying much. When Javier and his parents came to our house to officially ask for my hand in marriage, my mother called me to her room to speak to me. She asked me if I liked Javier. I told her I loved him. I thought that she was being old fashioned and that she was substituting the word like for love, I felt that as she had been married for so many years she had forgotten what it was like to be in love. She looked at me and said "No, I mean do you like him? You have to like the person you are going to spend the rest of your life with, you have to like and respect him because as the years go by when you no longer feel butterflies in your stomach when he walks into the room you are in, you have to like what is left."

"When your father approached me as I was out with my friends in the *Feria de Abril*[15] I turned him down, his brothers and himself had a *Don Juan* like reputation and I wanted nothing to do with the likes of such men. I wanted a

---

[15] Feria de Abril/Feria de Sevilla is the name given to the yearly main local festivities of Sevilla. It is a very colourful event, where people gather to celebrate and there is abundant food, wine, music, exhibitions, horse driven carriages...Almost everyone is dressed in the typical regional dress which has had very little variation through the years. Visitors come from various parts of the world to participate in this singular activity.

good, humble, serious, church going man, just like my father. He kept coming to court me, bringing a lot of expensive gifts for my family, coming into our very humble home and spending hours with them, there were times when I even left him there and went out just to show him that he wasn't welcome in my home. I told him that he had all the characteristics in a man that I was not looking for, he was just wasting his time and the sooner he accepted it, the better for him. He had so many women after him, all the mothers were taking their daughters, dressed in their finest, to every *feria* or event they knew he would be at. I felt that he was persistent because of my lack of interest; I was a challenge to him. I really did not want to marry him; I was convinced that he would make me really miserable if I did. But, my mother started encouraging me, I don't know why, she knew the same things I did, she had advised me all my life to stay away from such men but she told me that she had seen something in him. Because I trusted her judgement, I still don't know why, but I accepted his proposal and for me, love came after marriage. That was when I really fell in love with your father, the butterflies in my stomach came after I married him, I really liked the man that was left after all the pretty wrappings had been torn off and thrown away. He is a good, solid man and through the years he has been my support. That is what you should look for too, at the end of the day, nothing else matters."

"As you can see, I still remember every word she said to me that day, it was a story my brothers and I had heard so many times from both my parents and their families. Somehow, on this occasion, she was trying to tell me something, she wanted me to stop and think and see if I liked what was beneath all the glamour. I didn't understand what she meant, of course I liked Javier, he was clever, funny, handsome... What more could I want? Now, I know exactly what she intended to convey with her words and the answer to that question is... No. I don't like Javier, I loathe him. How can I come back from this, I have no idea. What should I do?"

"First of all, I need to stress that you are in an extremely dangerous situation. I think you need to alert your family and let them know what is going on, it's not a burden for one person to carry. From what you tell me his parents are not helping you and whether you like it or not, this has become a matter for the police."

"I can't do that. My parents would be incredibly hurt, I can't let them know what has been going on. Javier's therapist told me that the fact that I didn't leave him has given him a reason to make an effort and control himself, if I go, I feel I will be responsible for whatever he does to someone else if he discontinues his treatment but I don't love him. When I look at him I feel fear, resentment, pity...

but not love. Is this what the rest of my life is going to be? I'm only twenty-nine."

"You say you are not a good person and yet a lot of your actions are to protect others. I must insist you alert your family and should anything else happen, go to the police. There are too many women who are killed because they opted for silence out of shame or fear. I don't want you to become just another statistic."

"My parents are devoted to each other, they go everywhere together and my father is a man feared and respected by many but he always comes home to consult my mother when he has to make an important decision. If I were to divorce Javier without giving a reason, I feel my father who isn't a religious man would accept it but for my mother, marriage is a lifelong commitment and I if I have to choose between seeing the disappointment on her face and staying with Javier, I think I prefer the latter option."

"It is clear that your family means a lot to you but I can assure you that a mother's love knows no bounds and your family would rather have you alive and safe than living in that kind of terror and hopelessness. You need to come to terms with the fact that you are in an abusive relationship, you have suffered extreme cruelty and I don't even know if this marriage is valid as your husband seems to have broken almost every vow he made to you on your wedding day. The case would have to be studied, we have experts in this field and I can help you whatever you decide to do but don´t hesitate to go to the authorities should you feel you are in any form of danger."

"Don´t you think he can change?"

"Human beings have an incredible capacity to inflict pain and suffering on others and some people derive pleasure from this. I don´t know Javier personally, I want to believe that with adequate medication and therapy he can lead a normal life but I have to exercise caution, in the five years that I have been a priest, I have seen a number of victims of domestic abuse and I have had the opportunity to speak to their abusers, some of them have made me feel that I was in the presence of pure and unadulterated evil. A lot of people have brain lesions but most of them don´t systematically beat up their wives, I don´t know if that is the explanation for everything that he has done to you. Something doesn´t add up or seem right to me."

"I am a man of faith and you are in a church, so I can tell you, even though you have stopped believing, that the deep remorse that is needed for a real change to occur has to come from a place and state of mind that most of these men don´t even know exists. I believe in forgiveness and redemption but you have to really want them. I truly hope I´m wrong and that your husband is not one of the many who have no real desire to make amends. On the other hand if you stay in this marriage, you need to really forgive him, put it all behind you and make a fresh start, you can´t have so many negative feelings for someone and not address them, they won´t get better with time, believe me."

"I can´t right now, I can´t forgive him. He has taken me to the darkest place I´ve ever been to, I have lost the ability to feel almost anything, my self esteem has never been lower, I have questioned everything, even felt I deserved it. Sometimes I feel like I´m losing my mind."

"True forgiveness is not always easy, sometimes letting go is the most difficult thing to do, but you are sitting in a place where everything is actually forgiven and slates are wiped clean all the time. You don´t have to do everything on your own. I have to get ready for mass but I will keep you both in my prayers, and please end the cycle of silence today, you are really not doing yourself any favours. These doors are always open; whenever you want to come in, use them."

I watch him get up and leave, I feel drained of energy, like I have completely emptied myself, which I actually have. I go outside where Juan is waiting to take me home. I come out feeling like I still have no answers, I don´t know what to do, before Javier told me about his blackouts I was certain that I was going to leave him and I felt relieved because I knew that it would be over soon but now I feel that if he wasn't to blame, if he didn't know what he was doing, then maybe he has been a victim of his circumstances. Maybe one day all these horrible feelings will go away and I will love him again. Should I stay?

    I have been going once a week with Javier to his therapy sessions, the psychologist has explained it all to me, the sudden outburst of rage, his inability to control them and the fact that he can't remember a lot of things that have happened. Everything seems to have a logical explanation.

TWENTY-TWO

BALOU

Today is my birthday, I'm told I'm a year old. To me, it feels like I'm a seventy, with all that has happened. I get lots of kisses and cuddles from Rosario who has wrapped a number of boxes, which she opens for me one by one while she utters exclamations and claps her hands... I don't know why, when she knows what's in each of them as she bought and wrapped them herself, but let's go with it. I love boxes, so I inspect them all, lie on them, jump into them and lick the sticky tape, which she keeps removing from my reach. I have new balls, a new cat tree which Marcos is assembling, a cat bed, blanket, treats and boxes. I quickly sit on the biggest one so it isn't thrown away, they have a tendency to do away with them after they have served their purpose. Rosario says she doesn't know why she bothered when it is evident what I liked best. I wish the house was full of boxes of different sizes, I would be so happy going in and out of them, biting the edges, sleeping in them, hiding and surprising innocent passersby... The list of what I could do is just endless.

I go and visit Adela, who puts a saucer of ice cream down on the floor, it's vanilla, which is my favourite. She winks at me and tells me it would be our secret, that woman really knows how to brighten up my day. When I finish, I go out to look for Juan so he can lift me on his shoulder to see if I can get at one of the birds that are usually hanging from the tree branches, they taunt me constantly. So far I have only been able to catch one which I decided to present to Rosario, a gesture to cheer her up, the kind you make to people you really care about. I placed it on her pillow next to her head while she was asleep. I was excited waiting for her to wake up and praise my skills as a hunter. When I saw her open her eyes, I puffed up my chest ready to accept without shame all the recognition that was due to me, only to hear her emit a blood curdling scream. Marylin rushed in while she pointed to the dead bird and at the same time, moving as far away from it as possible. What did she expect? That it would be alive after I had played with it the whole night? To my great shock and amazement she ordered it to be buried outside. I found her response to my thoughtful gift extremely ungrateful and I sulked for the rest of day.

Relations seem to be a bit better between Javier and Rosario, once a week they leave together and sometimes when they meet in the drive way they exchange a few pleasantries. I keep my distance from that man, from what I have learnt in our daily staff meetings in the kitchen, he is like that because he sustained a head injury in a car accident. In my opinion he was born that way, there is no cure for that. It seems that he is trying to fix himself so now he has all the employees feeling sorry for him, sometimes I wonder if we all witnessed the same event or if I´m living in a parallel reality from the rest of them.

When we happen to cross paths, I stare at him as I walk by. He needs to know that he will never, ever, be in my good books, I run a very selective club. It´s only open to people who don´t throw me across a room with the intent to cause me harm. At least he hasn´t attempted to touch me again. I on the other hand fantasise about ways of getting rid of him all the time, running in between his legs when he is walking... especially when he is just at the top of the staircase...

He doesn't receive visitors, the only person that comes to see him, is his mother, I have discovered that she is the one feeding him and taking care of the cleaning and maintenance of the pool house.

I am never usually let near the gates as there is a general fear that I might escape to the big wide world outside. The truth is that it holds absolutely no appeal for me, after having been confined to that glass cubicle in the pet shop; I am quite content with the house and its impressive gardens. So each time, I start to walk down the driveway that leads to the massive metal gates separating and protecting me from the many dangers that lie in wait outside, two strong hands normally pick me up and take me back inside, the owner of the hands varies, but the action is always the same. Even though there is a cat flap and I can come and go as I want, orders have been given to the security men near the main gate that I should be escorted back to the house should I venture too near.

But on this occasion, Juan is called into the house to collect some documents and I dart towards the security booth next to the entrance. I want to surprise Diego who works there during the day, we have taken a liking to each other but I don´t normally have the opportunity to see him, other than when he is making his daily rounds of the grounds. He is sitting down behind a desk in the small room listening to the radio and I jump on to the table to say a proper "hello".

He pats my head and scratches me behind my ears, so I´m kind enough to offer him the underside of my chin so he can continue, just as I settle down, purring away, we hear a car horn outside, he gets up to see who it is, so I follow him... Apart from when I'm taken to the vet and I'm usually inside my carrier, I want to see what is so special about the world outside that all the rest get to see every day and make a special effort for me not to.

A man in uniform gets down from the driver's seat and hands Diego two big bags.

"This is for Don[16] Javier, from his mother, please make sure he gets it. Tell him that it's food and his laundry."

"Of course, thank you."

The man leaves and I get closer to the road, I look around me and I see there are similar gates to ours on either side of the house. I wonder if there are more cats around and just as I'm putting my left paw forward to go and inspect the house to the right, I am scooped up from the ground.

"No, no, no... You can't be here, I could get into very serious trouble if someone saw you. Come on, let's go in."

He escorts me back into the house where Adela decides I've been out enough for one day and she closes the

---

[16] Formal title used before a first name. *Don* for a male and *Doña* for a female.

cat flap. This really doesn't bother me because like I have mentioned there is a lot to entertain me and to keep me busy in the house,

 I'm sitting next to one of the big windows overlooking the front garden, I'm waiting for Rosario to come home. I know it's almost time for her to arrive and I'm watching so I can greet her as she opens the door, she loves me to be the first thing she sees when she comes in and usually she makes a big fuss of me. She gets out of the car and starts walking towards me, just as I'm about to jump down from the window sill to take my position by the door so she can act all surprised to see me... I see something catches her attention and she turns. It is Javier coming towards her. They stand close and talk and I see her smile and just before she turns around to leave, he touches her shoulder. I notice that she does not draw away or keep the safe distance like she has done for some time.

 The next morning, twelve red roses arrive for her; she reads the card and hides it in her dressing gown pocket and asks Marylin to put them in a flower vase on the table in the hall, I can guess who they are from... "Somehow" the vase falls off the table and shatters, all the contents have to be thrown away. I watch on with some detachment while I start grooming myself.

--

TWENTY-THREE

ROSARIO

    Balou and my work have been what have kept me from losing my sanity these past months when I touched rock bottom. Everything seemed so chaotic and disorganised, I felt like I had no control over my life, I hated the feeling it left me with, everything was so muddled up, I just couldn´t think straight. As Javier asked, I started going to therapy with him once a week and little by little this has helped me see him in a different light, I observe just how vulnerable he is and how little he is also in control of his actions, he says he hates the consequences they have had. He goes everyday to therapy and is taking medication to help stabilize his mood swings. One of the reasons I´m also attending therapy is because I want everything to be over as quickly as possible, but the things I'm learning are really surprising me and I have to admit that I'm not as indifferent as I thought I would be, but at the moment it's not something I want to analyse.

I am in sitting, lost in my thoughts when I hear the voice of Dr. Álvarez addressing me.

"Now that things have calmed down a little and that you have more information regarding both your situations. Can you share your thoughts with us?"

Both men are looking at me, waiting for my answer and I have no idea what they expect me to say. I'm coming to terms with the fact that there is a reason for what happened, that it wasn't my fault, that maybe Javier was telling the truth about loving me more than his life but the memory of each blow I received through the last five years are still extremely vivid in my mind.

"I understand all that the different doctors we have visited, yourself and Javier have explained, but I don't know what is expected of me, I feel like you both want everything to go away, just by sitting down and talking about things. Like everything that has happened in the last five years can be erased with words. The truth is that I don't think I can ever look at Javier the way I once did, we are both too damaged and broken and I don't want to spend my life looking over my shoulder, wondering when he will raise his hands to me again or counting his pills to make sure that he has taken them every day. I feel under a lot of pressure too..."

"Why don´t you tell Javier exactly what you want?"

I look at Dr. Álvarez, wondering if he heard anything I just said. I come to therapy to help Javier´s recovery because it´s easier to play along, but I have absolutely no intention of being analysed by anyone, nor do I feel the need to share my deepest thoughts with them. For that, I have Padre Antonio, from time to time I go and sit in the quiet of the church because it reminds me of a part of my life I would give anything to go back to and it has become my safe haven. I sit in peace, without feeling the pressure of the expectations of everyone around me. I know that my staff do not approve of the fact that Javier and I seem to be on better terms, even Balou shows his disapproval, loud and clear, sometimes a bit too loud. So it´s the one place that I feel alone with my thoughts, Padre Antonio when he passes by my side, stops to say hello and I seize the opportunity to open up to him as I feel that all this is leading up to me taking Javier back into my life and my home and I´m at this point, torn. So I face Javier and I look into his eyes, I see fear, sorrow and anxiety.

"I don´t hate you anymore but I don´t love you and I don´t know what it is that I want at the moment, I´m focused on trying to help you get better but I can't erase everything that has happened just because there is a reason for it. With every insult, unkind word, blow, little by little you succeeded in killing my illusions, my hopes, my dreams... I am now a different woman from the one you married and not a better one. You´ve taken a lot from me and you can´t give it back no matter how much you try."

"I know that and I´m grateful for your time and help, I really can´t bear the thought of you leaving with so much bitterness. Whatever you decide to do, I will accept it, I won´t make things difficult for you, but I won´t pretend that I don´t love you just to make it easier for you to walk away."

"You have spoken about everything, your past, feelings, regrets... But what about Eva, how do you intend making it up to her?"

Javier looks up in shock as I mention her name and the room goes silent, it´s as if both men have stopped breathing.

"Yes, I know about her, I wasn´t the first woman to suffer your wrath. I have met her, seen what you turned her into and in all these years, you never even bothered to check on her. Did you tell the good doctor this too? Because showing remorse and saying how sorry you are is too easy.

Actions always speak louder than words, as they say, and you have done nothing. So when you talk about love, I find it very difficult to understand how you can cause someone you say you love so much, all that pain. I spoke to that young woman and you are the cause of all her misfortunes, you destroyed her life and then you proceeded to build one with me, without even giving her another thought."

Dr. Álvarez looks at Javier who seems deep in thought. I wait for a reply from either of them, some form of justification that can somehow fix it all but I fear that there is no easy solution to this.

"He told me about her, he was open about everything he did, it was necessary for me to be able to help him move on and to have all the information."

"That incident happened just after my accident, until my parents called me to tell me that they had found her, I had no recollection of what had occurred. I tried to find her... to give, I don´t know what form of explanation, but she seemed to have vanished into thin air. How did you find her?"

"Through your mother. I met Eva at a café and talked about all that had happened. To date, she still does not understand what took place and she blames herself. I sat there listening and feeling sorry for her, when I have been more the fool. I let you systematically do the same to me for years and she doesn´t know that she was the lucky one. If I found her, then you could have done the same if you had really wanted to, but it´s easier to close your eyes and pretend like nothing ever happened."

"Yes, I did try, but not hard enough. I convinced myself that she was fine, she would be married with children and she would have forgotten all about me, but now that I´m trying to put right all the wrongs I have done, I need to start with her. Can you give me her contact details? I have to make amends. I know my parents gave her a lot of money but I need to man up and accept my responsibilities."

"I´ll ask her if she wants to see you and I´ll let you know."

Two days later, I call Eva and ask her if she would like to talk with Javier and explain that he has requested to see her. She agrees and I set up a meeting in one of our board rooms at the office. I leave them to talk as I feel like an intruder in their story and her pain. About an hour later, Javier comes in to say he is leaving, he looks worn out and sad. I go in to see how Eva is and I find her crying and looking out of a window. I don´t know what to do as it is such an unusual situation, so I stand by her side in silence.

"It wasn´t my fault, it wasn´t my fault..."

I look at her as she repeats the words because I know exactly how she feels and I sense that through the years, she must have replayed the incident over and over in her mind, trying to find some sort of explanation.

"No, it was not your fault at all."

"Thank you for arranging the meeting, you were the last person I expected help from, the wife of the man I lo... I needed to understand, an apology, anything to give me some insight and a reason not to sink deeper into my depression."

I know what she was about to say, she loves Javier because in all this time, she has somehow found a way to excuse his behaviour and now that she knows that it was something he couldn't help doing, she must be thinking that if she had known, then she could have helped him and they still would be together. She wishes she were in my shoes, little does she know that I would not wish anyone to be walking in them. She had a very lucky escape. I can read all the emotions on her face, she is one of those people that can't hide what she is thinking.

"It was the least I could do, I just wish it had never happened, you have spent such a long time feeling sorry for yourself, you deserve so much more in life but more especially, the chance to be happy. What would you like to do now?"

--

"I have absolutely no idea, I hardly go out, I just spend as much time as possible behind closed doors, it's where I feel safe, far away from prying eyes. I have become a recluse as the medication for my depression combined with stuffing myself with food to combat my anxiety have turned me into someone I can't even recognise or like when I look in the mirror. I haven't worked in seven years, I didn't even finish my university degree. I don't know if I will ever lead a normal life or be good around people again, I've become quite anti-social. Too many years of silence have made me withdrawn as I couldn't tell anyone what happened and those around me were full of questions. My family has watched me become what I am today without understanding the reason why."

"Look, I've just given my personal assistant a few days off as she recently lost her mother and she isn't coping well with her grief at all. If you want to work here till she returns, I would gladly have you. You will have an office adjoining mine, so this will help if you don't want to see people or you feel overwhelmed, you need to take baby steps and join the living once again."

"Oh, no, no, no, I wouldn't know what to do...I don't think I can."

I read the panic in her eyes, the thought of going back into the real world, having to interact with people... I know I need to be cruel to be kind. If she doesn't do this, or something similar, things won't get better, she would only withdraw more and more into her shell and finally, completely lose herself because it's much the easier option.

"Eva, do you want to be a victim all your life? Let someone-else's actions condition and destroy you completely? You aren't even thirty yet, is this what it's going to be like day after day? I'm offering you the opportunity of a new start, without stress or the pressure of a regular job, you can leave if it's too much for you but I urge you to at least give it a try. I want you to think long and hard about your future, you have an opportunity to rewrite it, for better or for worse, Javier has moved on and you really need to do the same thing."

I leave her with those words...

I know that I should have applied them to myself a long time ago. Lately, everything I do reminds me of what I should have done.

TWENTY-FOUR

BALOU

I am sitting on my high stool beside Adela in one of our meetings, apart from analysing the situation of their master´s, I have learnt a lot about the personal lives of the four members of our little group; they now have more time to talk to each other, their common enemy has given them a reason to.

Marylin and Marcos have been married for twenty years and they have three children that remained behind in the Philippines, they are in the care of their paternal grandmother. Every month, they send them money for their up-keep, they talk about them a lot and miss them very much, but they explained that the situation was unsustainable for them in their country and that they chose to sacrifice not seeing their children in order to give them a better future than the one they had. Marcos explained that the Filipino community is quite large in Madrid as a lot of them had come to Spain with the same objective, so on weekends when they are free, they gather with some of their compatriots as it makes them feel closer to their home. I took a look at the photographs they showed the others of their children and I have to say, "It´s a good thing they take after their mother".

Adela talks about her children and her late husband all the time. She misses him a lot as she says that children have to live their lives and when the time comes, they need to be independent and leave the nest. She tells us that she started working after he died because she couldn´t bear the emptiness and silence of her home. I look at her when she speaks of this and I can sense the great sadness in her, the void that she feels with the absence of the person she thought she would grow old with, because of this, I´m always extra nice to her, she knows I understand her. She is the oldest of the four and very motherly, she just seems to exude homeliness and comfort. Always trying to put some flesh on to all our bones, something I really appreciate.

Juan is the youngest of them all and his personal life is always of interest to the rest, especially the two women. They keep urging him to settle down with a nice girl. He seems to have a few candidates as they call him sometimes when he is with us. He is asked to explain who they are, but I suspect and I think so does Adela, even though she has never said anything in front of him, that he has a soft spot for Rosario. I can't blame him because she is simply beautiful, even when she has been at her worse, her face disfigured and looking small and hurt, there is something about her. It's just a pity they didn't meet earlier, they would have been perfect together and Rosario does not look like the kind of woman who would not marry a lowly chauffeur. Now that she seems to have a firmer grip on her life, I see that she is the kind of person that has a strong personality; I sense certain strength underneath that keeps struggling to surface. Every day, I watch her gain more and more confidence in herself, the way she dresses, the way she looks and the way she is now standing tall and upright, she no longer jumps up in fright when she hears a sudden noise. She has a commanding presence and I am seeing a side of her that I hadn't seen before and I like it, I'm finally meeting the real Rosario. When I first saw her, I sensed fear, a great sadness, it was like she wanted to make herself as small as possible and crawl into a hole where no one could find her, she spent her days in bed, but now, as each day passes, I feel her growing in confidence. I want to say that I'm proud of her and happy for her but I'm sceptical about the fact that "Cold Eyes" has something to do with this change. I would have given anything for her to have walked away and found herself far from him but life has a way of not giving me what I want.

We have all seen them grow closer together, little by little, the flowers and gifts he sends, the tickets to one function or the other, the talks in the garden, the way she does not pull her hand away any more...

At first everyone was dead set against it, especially after seeing the extent of what he had done to her but now I also see a change in their attitudes and opinions towards him. So today, after Adela has settled them all down with a cup of coffee and a grilled sandwich and of course some ham for me, we all proceed to analyse the situation. They do all the talking; I just digest all the information.

"Well, I know it's early days yet but I feel it's only a matter of time before Don Javier comes back into the house."

I look at Marylin when she says this, "Don Javier" it's now "Don Javier" when not so long ago, it was "that man" or "the monster". How is it possible that everyone is seeing something different from what I see?

"Yesterday he sent her a breakfast basket, you know the kind that comes with tea, coffee, jam, a mug, a flask, ham, olive oil, ground tomatoes, biscuits... not that I looked to closely of course, she smiled when she received it. I would have broken that man's head myself had he laid another finger on her but now that I know that he had a medical condition and that he is getting treatment, he deserves a second chance. It's just like when soldiers come back from the war, some of them have problems and they can't adapt to real life because of traumas they sustained there. They need to be given help and support. I'm just happy to see the change in her, no longer hiding in her room, normally I would advise that in such serious cases of domestic abuse the victim runs as far as possible from the attacker, but this proves that people can actually change and he is making such an effort, plus he is such a handsome man too."

Incredible! Even Adela who called him a long list of names that I can't even put into writing each time she spoke of him, is all about starting a new chapter, you can tell that she is a romantic woman as each of the gestures Javier has made towards Rosario brings a dreamy look into her eyes. The only people who do not seem to share their great joy are Juan and Marcos, they remain quiet while the women nod and smile as they recount all the good things they now see; they are even talking about having babies in the not too distant future. What is becoming clear to me is that women seem to be hopeless romantics, it just clouds their judgment.

"Well, let's see how things go before you two start planning a baptism."

Juan smiles at them as he gets up to leave and I see him and Marcos exchange a glance.

TWENTY-FIVE

ROSARIO

If someone had told me five months ago that I would be smiling while reading a note Javier pushed under the door, I would wonder which drug they were on. I can't believe the change that both Javier and myself have experienced. I'm not the same person that I was before all this started, I have lost my innocence, but I honestly thought that there was no way on earth I could actually ever look at him again and not be filled with negative feelings or that I would be counting the days until I could walk out the door for good. But listening to him week after week, talking about his life, feelings, hopes, while we both attend the therapy sessions, the way he has struggled to turn things around and the way he looks at me. I feel like I don´t know what to think anymore.

We talk a lot, go for walks, go to the movies, the theatre, dinner, he buys me flowers and sends me notes. It´s just like in the beginning only with the knowledge of the past which will help us not to make the same mistakes again. He hasn´t asked us to be more than friends yet and I am grateful for that, it helps me not feel the pressure of having to make a decision yet. Even the staff seem to view things from a different perspective, Adela and Marylin look forward to the surprise of the day with the same illusion as I do, so of course they share in all the flowers, chocolates, breakfast baskets...

The only one who does not seem at all thrilled is Balou, he still hisses each time Javier comes near him or for that matter me and now that my little black panther is older and bigger, it is quite impressive to see; he looks really angry when he does this. Javier has bought him toys and treats; he tries to hand feed the latter to him but the cat will not go near him of his own accord. When I´m home, we spend all our time together, he loves being by my side and on my shoulder, although he has become quite heavy now I still don´t mind. I love hearing him purr while we walk around the house as he views his surroundings from a different height He loves playing hide and seek and likes me to chase him, he comes charging in when I peek at him from a corner of the door. He is a very funny creature and has to make no effort at all to put a smile on my face. I just wish he would give Javier a chance.

Concha has been taking care of Javier all this while, she made sure he had food, clean clothes and that the pool house is in order by sending someone three times a week to clean up. They have kept all that happened a secret from his father, Javier has explained that he would never forgive him if he knew, he apparently made it clear that he would take him out of this world if he had to as he himself had come from an abusive family situation and it had scarred him for life. She popped in to see me the other day on her way out from visiting Javier. I looked up from the book I was reading because Balou raised his head from my stomach, where he had been taking a nap; I see her stand hesitantly in the doorway to the parlour.

"I just came to say hello, I know that we haven´t spoken since the last time you came to see me and it was a very tense meeting. I really didn´t think things would ever get any better."

"Please take a seat, would you like a glass of "*Horchata*"[17] it´s really hot today."

"No, I´m fine. I just had lunch with Javier and I couldn´t possibly eat anything else. The cat is huge now."

"Yes he is, getting bigger and finer every day."

I know we both remember that she wanted me to put him to sleep the last time we met and I see she chooses not to sit too close to us. But she need not worry; Balou does not approach people who do not show interest in him. He is a very comfortable cat and to prove it, he has gone back to sleep after looking Concha up and down and deciding she has nothing to offer him.

"I have wanted to apologise to you for so long now, I said some really horrible things the last time we saw each other, there was no excuse for my behaviour. I have been waiting with bated breath since everything happened. I expected things to explode at any moment and I would be torn between my son and my husband, not wanting to find out who I would decide to stand by. But you have really surprised me, I didn´t expect so much help from you towards Javier, when you had every reason not to."

---

[17] A refreshing drink made from water, sugar and ground tiger nuts, originally from Valencia and usually served with *Fartons*.

"I guess guilt has a lot to do with it, if I didn't have the image of my parents constantly present in my thoughts or feel the need to make them feel proud of me at all times, I'd have had no qualms about walking away."

"I haven't seen him so happy in such a long time, I just didn't think..."

Her voice breaks and she looks away and so do I. She is a proud woman and being one myself, I know that we do not like showing weakness to others. I sit up, gently putting Balou on the sofa while he utters a meow of protest for the interruption of his sleep and I offer her a tissue. She takes a deep breath.

"I'm sorry it just seemed like things could only get worse and I was so scared of my son going to jail and our family name being dragged through the mud on every television programme with all our friends looking the other way when they'd see us..."

I nod my head while I listen, truth be told if this ever came out, it would be the end of them because our society is very unforgiving. A lot of people get close to you because of what they can get out of you or the prestige they get from the association. It's true that their family is very powerful at the moment but all that would be wiped out and forgotten in a single second, it just takes one bad act for all the good to be erased.

"And maybe you might get together again."

"That's something that we haven't considered yet, right now, it's enough that we are comfortable again in each other's company."

"Well, I just wanted to thank you for being a bigger person than I was. I have to go now, I have an auction to attend and there is a painting I need to get my hands on."

We give each other two kisses and she leaves while I try not to imagine which horrendous work of art she is about to spend a lot of money on.

TWENTY-SIX

BALOU

Things have not at all gone in the direction I wanted or hoped for, a week ago, "that man" moved back into the house. Juan and I watched from the garden while his things were moved back by Marylin and Marcos and you could tell that we both felt that it was not a giant step forward for mankind. This was a disaster waiting to happen.

Adela and Marylin were of course ecstatic because for them, it seemed like the happy ending to a very difficult story; Adela was especially glad, because their being back together meant she had more work, she often said "It's no fun cooking for just one person", so now she could go back to cooking for them both and also for friends, apparently, in the beginning, when everything was perfect, they entertained a lot. She brought out her cookery books and magazines and she spent a lot of time pouring over them and writing down things on her note pad.

I will miss spending countless hours with her in the back garden, she created it with so much love, it's full of herbs and her favourite vegetables. She always includes them in her recipes as she often says, "nothing enhances a dish better than home grown organic ingredients." So as Rosario is not a breakfast person, we put a lot of time into our favourite outdoor activity, well she would weed, water and plant and I'd just let Mr. Sun pamper me while I stretched out full length on the stepping stones. It just wasn't the same doing this on my own without someone making a fuss over me once in a while with the excuse of taking a short break. I soon found that sitting down watching her produce endless batches of muffins, cakes and bread was just as good an alternative. The mixture of smells that emanated from the kitchen was enough to keep me constantly interested in what was going on.

Marylin did complain that she had more work though, as now she had to iron all his shirts, he changed twice a day... but apart from that everyone seemed happy at the way things had turned out. The only one who lost out in "the great move" was me... I was no longer allowed to sleep with Rosario, with the pretext that I made too much noise and it was impossible to get a good night's rest, every night when it was time to turn out the lights, I was gently put out onto the landing by Rosario. I didn't see what the problem was, before "Cold Eyes" came back into the house, the noise I made was cute, now it is annoying. The root of the problem is clear to me.

I don't want to seem unfeeling, it is actually great to see Rosario walk with a spring in her step and laugh out loud, she really seems happy and I have to say that except with me, I had never seen her the same way with anyone else. We still spend a lot of time together so I can't really complain.

Javier has tried to make his peace with me, each time he sees me, he tries to pat my head but I shrink away. I know it makes Rosario unhappy and that she would like me to make more of an effort to get along with him but I only do things that come natural to me and that require little effort, I'd really have to go out of my way to like him so it's really not worth my while.

I walk into the kitchen for my breakfast and Adela and Rosario are excitedly talking and writing things down.

"Adela are you sure you can cope? I really don't mind ordering the food from a catering company. Cooking for twenty people is a lot of work. Anyway, I have hired two waiters to serve dinner."

"Of course I can, I was born to do this, I love cooking and I have already made the Russian salad, it´s in the fridge. I´m about to start with the stuffing for the turkey, then I´ll do the *Gazpacho*[18]. Once the turkey is in the oven, I´ll begin with the other starters and side dishes. I have cooked for my large family when we come together for Christmas, so many times. This is just like a walk in the park. I am just happy that you are throwing this party for your friends. This is what you should be doing, having fun. You deserve it."

"I know what you mean, I´ve spent so long hiding from them, I just want them back in my life. I´m just really glad that everything seems to be falling into place, it´s a new beginning and I´m so excited about it. My group of friends from Sevilla, where I grew up, have travelled all the way here to be with me. I haven´t seen them in such a long time."

I´m sitting on the window sill and I´m taking all the information in, I now understand why Marylin and Marcos are cleaning and polishing everything in the sitting rooms and the big dining room and why Adela has a look of sheer joy on her face. Juan has been bringing in bags and bags of groceries all

---

[18] Cold tomato based soup which is very typical in Southern Spain. There are some variations to it depending on the region.

morning. I spent some time trying to get into some of them but Adela threatened to ban me from the kitchen, so I decided to sit quietly and watch from afar. It was fascinating seeing the dexterity with which she chopped and cut, the finished dishes were all covered and put into the three big fridges. I spent the whole day by her side, while Rosario went about getting herself ready, she had her hair and nails done, she was looking fabulous and from time to time she came in to supervise what was going on in our department.

Finally everything is ready, it had been a very long but satisfying day, especially as I am offered a taste of practically everything, I feel like I´m bursting at the seams but I'm one very happy cat.

Soon we start hearing the sound of cars coming into the compound and parking up, then the voices of people greeting each other and laughing. The two waiters come into the kitchen and start preparing drinks ready to start serving them while Adela deftly arranges trays and trays of ham and shrimp cocktails for them to pass around before the guests go into the dining room. Earlier on, I had taken a look at what Marylin and Marcos had done with the place and it looked really beautiful, I then proceeded to inspect it at close quarters by jumping on the table but I was quickly returned back to the kitchen where I was reported to Adela who told me to stay with her, as it was where I was most wanted.

Juan is also having a very busy night as he is in charge of parking the cars properly, it is a good thing that the grounds are really big and there was a lot of space to do that. He also made it crystal clear that he didn't want me around as he was afraid that with so much movement I might get under a moving car, which I'm guessing would not be a good experience for me.

Empty trays and glasses keep coming into the kitchen and Marylin loads the dishwasher. The door is kept shut and the waiters have been told to be careful with me but there is so much going on that they can't keep an eye on me all the time, no one notices when I slip out to see what all the noise is about. There are a lot of people standing and chatting, I have never seen so many people in the house in all the time I had been here, everyone looks so elegant, the men are wearing suits and the women long dresses. Rosario is standing with three other women and they are all talking, shouting and laughing at the top of their voices. Javier is with a man and a woman at the other end of the room, most of the guests have a drink in their hands and they are taking food from the trays that the waiters are passing around. I decide to walk into the room and when I do, there is a silence as people turn to look at me. I move towards Rosario who picks me up and introduces me to her friends, just as I had expected, they all say how incredibly handsome I am while I proudly puff out my chest and enjoy all the attention. By this time my absence has been noted in the kitchen and Marcos is standing close by to collect me. I don't mind as I have made myself known to all and have been fussed about in the process. Mission accomplished.

I join the staff in the kitchen while they have their dinner. Earlier on, I had heard Rosario insist that Adela cooks a bit more of everything as she wants them to have the same food as the guests. They have set the table and are sitting down to eat; it looks like everyone is having a great time. For the first time in my life, I'm actually unable to eat anything more and this upsets me. I smell the ham Juan is offering me but turn away as I can't possibly eat another morsel. They all laugh at me. Adela made two turkeys, a smaller one for the staff and the larger one for the guests; it looks great, all brown and crispy. When the waiters take it in, I can hear the exclamations from the guest and Adela has gone a deep shade of red while the others smile at her and congratulate her.

The party goes on till the early hours of the morning and I go out into the garden to watch the last guest leave as Rosario and Javier wave them goodbye. He has his arm on her waist and she is leaning on his shoulder. I look at them and in all honesty, I have to say that they are the picture of contentment.

TWENTY-SEVEN

ROSARIO

I really can't explain what or how it happened. One minute I was feeling less threatened by Javier and trying to take in all that I had learnt about him and the next he was moving back in. It just happened without practically talking or thinking about it, it just seemed right. We had grown closer and closer and in ways that we had never been before. Not even when we were dating, before the nightmare began and everything had seemed so perfect.

His medication and attending weekly therapy sessions seemed to be helping him a lot; he was just a different person, as different as day and night. It looked like a weight had been lifted off his shoulders and I saw him laugh with abandon, something I wasn't sure I had ever seen him do before. Gone was that enigmatic smile that always left me wondering what he was thinking of. It was the way he treated me and made me feel like we were the only two people in the world, I felt really special. I have no idea when we got to the point when I could let go of my anger and resentment and actually see the man that I had fallen in love with more than five years ago... but I woke up one morning and I discovered that I felt exactly the same way as I did then and I knew that life was giving us a second chance. So when he asked me to start again and if we could wipe the slate clean, I said yes and this time, I wasn't scared or petrified for the future because something told me everything would be just fine.

I just felt incredibly happy and lucky, we started going out again and with that, the period of dryness with the press ended. Almost every week we would feature in one magazine or the other, going to concerts of classical music, for dinner, an event... I had worked so hard to keep my life away from them that it took me some time to get used to all that attention again.

We spent a lot of weekends travelling, we went to see my family in Sevilla, to Paris, Rome... It almost seemed wrong to be so happy but we had to make up for all the time we had lost. My family was so happy to see us, living in two different cities had been really good for me as I always found an excuse not to go when things were bad and they were also too busy to come over to Madrid, it had been a blessing in disguise. My mother told me that there was something different about me, she said I was glowing and asked if I had some good news for her, the poor woman thought that I was finally expecting a child and for the first time in such a long time, I was ready to start a family. We had talked about it and it just seemed right so I hoped I would be able to give her the good news in the near future.

It just seemed like for once everything was coming together, we were working hard in the Foundation and meeting our targets too. Pilar had come back to work and even though she had good and bad days, little by little, she was almost her former self. At first things were awkward with Eva as it was obvious that she was both grateful and resentful of me, getting back into a daily routine after so many years of inactivity and exiling herself from most of humanity was really difficult. But, everyday was a new start for her and by the time Pilar resumed her duties she was quite integrated in the team, I didn't want to let her go as she had made so much progress and I was afraid she would lose it all. I asked if she would like to work with Diego in the international project department and she agreed. I could see that she was also scared of what would become of her and of going back to her past life. I have watched her grow in confidence everyday and when I go to their office, Diego and her seem to stand a little bit too close, I smile to myself as I know that it will only be a matter of time before she opens her eyes and looks around her. Now they are preparing a trip to Peru to co-ordinate one of our projects there, I know that she is really excited about it, she hasn´t left the country in such a long time.

In all my confusion and when things were really bad, I would just go and sit in church because it was a place that made me feel safe; no explanations were required of me there. Padre Antonio just seemed relieved to see that I was alive, after seeing me a few consecutive days, just sitting at the back with my eyes closed, enjoying the quiet and peace in my mind, he told me that if I was to go there so often, then he had to put me to good use. I tried to explain that I was already working somewhere that did a lot of good in society but he told me I´d feel different after doing this.

He has put me in charge of the food bank the parish set up, with the economic crisis, a lot of families have lost their steady income, some have even lost their homes and a lot of people are finding it very difficult to make ends meet. So they decided that the parishioners would donate food, then twice a month, it is shared out between those that need it. What can I say? He was right, this is different. I go to the parish office two evenings a week to receive the donated food and also update the inventory. When people come in with a box of rice or sugar that they bought when they did their weekly shopping, it has a lot more meaning because they are also scraping to make ends meet. I have also got to know the families we help and it's really difficult to see people that once had a certain stability now struggling to come to terms with the fact that they have to depend on the good will of others, not everyone adapts well to their new situation. I accepted to do this because I'm grateful for all the time that Padre Antonio has spent listening to me over and over recounting the same story, but I'm surprised at what has been awakened in me. I see the big difference between sitting down behind a desk and making decisions or designing projects which are undeniably doing a lot of good for whole communities and actually working closely and helping the thirty families we cater for. I really feel like I'm actually making someone's world better.

I haven't found God yet... I know Padre Antonio and my mother are expecting me to do so any day now but I am grateful to him for the good people I have met lately who do have faith. The priest tells me, I'll wake up one morning and just decide to come back home, I laugh when he says this and we have long discussions and arguments about God and the Church. I really don't know if that will ever happen but I'm undeniably happier now than I have ever been in my whole life.

The only dark cloud in my horizon is due to the fact that the two males in my home can't seem to get along. Javier makes an effort but as soon as he comes near Balou, the latter moves away. It doesn't help that my husband does not want the cat in our room at night, he says he has to get up early and that the few times Balou has spent the night with us, he has woken up even more tired than when he went to bed. I guess I've got used to him jumping on me and waking me up at silly o'clock or when he decides to fight my feet under the duvet or give my face a midnight wash but I miss those things terribly. I know that if Balou gives Javier a chance, he will have another unconditional slave but I guess animals are less forgiving than humans.

--

TWENTY-EIGHT

ROSARIO

The day I have been dreading for months is finally here. I look at myself in the mirror while I adjust my coat with shaking hands, I try to button it but I seem not to be able to perform such an easy task. My mother comes up behind me and she hugs me, then proceeds to help me up, just like when I was a child. She looks up at me and smiles sadly.

"*Charo*[19], it´s time to go."

We go down the stairs where the staff, my father, brother and sister are waiting for us in silence. My father´s

---

[19] Popular and short version of the name Rosario.

driver opens the door of the car for us and my parents get in while I stand back for a second and watch Adela, Juan, Marcos and Marylin get into another car and my siblings into a third. I turn around and I see that Balou is watching us through the big glass door.

As we pass through the gates of the compound, we are blinded by the flashes from the cameras as our photographs are taken while paparazzi run after the car and reporters ask us to stop and answer questions, microphones in hand. I turn and see the black BMW behind us with the security team that my father has hired to keep people away from me. I look at both my parents, my mother is crying silently and looking through the window so no one will notice and my father is looking straight ahead, his jaw is clenched and I know that he is furious.

We arrive at the court house and immediately the car is once again surrounded by members of the press, I look up as if in a dream at the flashes and the video cameras that are recording every single second... Later it will be replayed time and time again. The four men in black suits that work for us start moving towards the car door, clearing a way for me to pass as my parents come to my side and shield me from all that is going on around me. I see my father push a reporter away and I know someone is going to pay for all the anger and impotence he is feeling at the moment. My mother quickly stands between him and the man and calls out my father's name various times until she is able to get his attention, they lock eyes for a second and she guides him towards us again. I am well aware that this is the price we have to pay for being one of the most powerful families in Europe. I have to admit that the press have been quite respectful, my family has never made money out of commercialising their personal lives, we have never given an interview as my father made it clear from the beginning that we weren't going to be known for anything other than our good name.

We are given the option of remaining in an adjoining room until it's our turn to testify or go into the court room, my father says he is going in, he tells my mother and I to stay behind. I look at him as he gets up and I follow him.

"I'm going with you, I didn't come all the way here just to wait for it to be over."

We go in and I see that all my family is seated; my uncles, aunts, cousins and best friends have all come from Sevilla to be with me at this moment when I need them most. I nod at them in greeting while we go and find a seat at the front next to Miguel and Soledad, my sister smiles at me and holds my hand, she doesn't let go till I have to get up to give evidence. The court room is full of people; there is not one empty seat. I look at the side of the accused and I see

Javier's parents Concha and Ernesto sitting right behind their son's two attorneys, I remember when she told me some time ago that she would destroy whichever testimony my staff took to court, they are both staring ahead and I don't see them exchange a single word throughout the proceedings. At that moment a side door opens and Javier walks in, he is handcuffed and led by a uniformed guard to his seat, he looks ahead when he passes in front of us. I shiver as if someone has just walked over my grave. The judge comes in and we are all asked to rise... when we sit back down the Clerk of the Court reads out the charges.

I really wonder what Javier's defence is going to come up with, this has been a very publicised case and he has been tried and put out to hang by the media and public opinion. Every time I switched on the television I had to change channels because I often encountered a group of people analysing my life and the events that had happened. The day Javier was arrested; we even made the headlines of the national news.

My mind escapes to what happened three months ago while my attorney introduces his first witness.

Things had been going so well, it had been six months since we got back together and if I say that we were happy, it would be an understatement.

Miguel had just graduated with honours from the University and Javier and I had talked about throwing him a party before he left for the USA just like I did to pursue a master's degree. I had invited my parents, sister and immediate family to come to Madrid. My mother came with my brothers a few days earlier so we could spend some more time together. We were all so proud of him and we were preparing a video with messages congratulating him and wishing him the best of luck from family and friends and were going to surprise him with it at the dinner party.

It was great having them around as with all that had happened and being so far away from each other we had spent very little time together. The women went out shopping and my mother and I worked with Adela planning the great evening. Miguel and Javier meanwhile kept busy watching sports on TV, playing tennis or going to the club, anything but coming into the kitchen with us.

On Saturday my father arrived with his two brothers and their families, they had not been able to come earlier due to professional commitments that they couldn't avoid. There was so much noise when they arrived, but noise of a good kind, the type that reminds you of good times in the past. My father immediately went for Balou and soon they were playing the cat's favourite game of "catch me if you can". It was funny watching them play; I had never seen my father with another animal that weren't his dogs or beloved horses. I would never have put him down as a cat person and Balou seemed to also be smitten by him, he abandoned my side as soon as he saw my father and stayed by him all day. During the day more cousins and my mother´s only sister, Mercedes, also arrived. It was just great to have them all under the same roof again.

At eight o´clock the few good friends we had invited from Madrid started arriving; among the guests were my parents-in-law too. We hired waiters to serve and help out Adela who was in her element; she lived for moments like these in which she had so many people to cook for. We all dressed for the occasion and everyone looked very elegant. The dining room was looking beautiful and we had set up the giant screen there for Miguel´s surprise. The meal was lovely, toasts were made, tears were shed, all by the proud women of the family, even though I saw my father´s eyes were glistening... We left my brother speechless when we showed him the video, it had cost a lot to prepare, exchanging endless emails with everyone until we got what we thought was perfection.

Balou was by my father´s side, his stool had been brought in from the kitchen and he tasted everything that passed through my father´s plate. I protested as I don´t like giving him human food but my father replied that he was helping him maintain his stout constitution and that the cat was in agreement with this arrangement.

I noticed Javier was unusually quiet during dinner but I assumed he was preoccupied with work, he was putting a lot of hours in on a project that he needed to complete in the coming days and this had him on edge, I heard him speak to his father about it as he was preparing him a drink. Once dinner was over, we all got up to take coffee and dessert in the lounge, as I made to move to be with the others, I was stopped by Marcos who told me that I had a phone call. I decided to pick it up in the study, away from the noise so I could hear properly. I went in and shut the door, it was from a good childhood friend, Ana; she wasn't able to make it but was calling to extend her congratulations to the family. I put the receiver down and turned around to see Javier standing right behind me. This scared me as I had not heard him come in, so I moved back and proffered a nervous laugh.

"You startled me, is everything all right?"

"Why shouldn´t it be?"

He had a very strange look on his face, one I couldn´t read but that I found strangely familiar, I don´t know why but as I took a step backwards and he took a step towards me, suddenly the reason for my discomfort became clear. I felt as if someone had struck me and the air had been let out of me. He was looking at me the same way; the way he used to just before he'd hit me. I turned and looked for an escape route and that was when I received a blow to the stomach. I let out an involuntary scream and doubled over. I needed to get out of there, I was conscious of the fact that my whole family was celebrating downstairs and the last thing I wanted was for them to find out. I held on to the high chair next to me for support while I clutched my stomach with the other hand, I looked at Javier, wondering what had happened, what had set him off? I didn't understand anything, he was taking his medication and they had helped till this moment to control his mood swings. I felt a chill as what I saw in his eyes a look of undisguised pure hatred. I tried to get past him and get to the door; I knew that he would control himself in front of the others but he grabbed my arm and started twisting it, I couldn't stand the pain and I fell to my knees while screaming in agony, hoping no one could actually hear me. I felt as if his intention was to break my arm or worse. I was crying and begging him to stop, when suddenly the door opened and my father charged in, he pushed Javier with such force that he fell on the floor and he then started hitting him. I heard screams as my mother's sister who was the first to arrive at the scene rushed to my aid; at the same time Javier's parents came in... I heard my mother let out an exclamation.

"Miguel stop, stop, you will kill him."

--

But my father was still hitting him so she went towards him and tried to push him away from the man lying on the floor, she called for help from my uncles. No one moved, they were all standing and watching, so she turned to my brother. By this time I had been helped by my aunt and sister on to the couch, I saw that the door had been shut by one of my uncles; my cousin was helping my mother and brother who were finally able to drag my father off Javier, whose face was now a bloody mess. My father reminded me of raging bull, every single vein in his face and neck were sticking out and he was breathing heavily. His brothers then took him out of the room as he seemed ready to finish what he started.

    I was watching everything from the safe place I normally went to when these things happened; from there it felt like I was seeing things occur to someone else, but as I felt the horrible pain shooting through my arm and shoulder, I was reminded that everything was real and once again, I was the main actress in the unending horror movie… a movie that just had too many sequels. What shocked me most was that Ernesto, my father-in-law did not intervene, he stood back the whole time while he watched as his son was beaten to within an inch of his life, I even saw him hold his wife back when she tried to move towards my father. My mother was crying beside me whilst trying not to hold me, as each time she forgot and tried to hug me, I screamed out in pain.

Within minutes a doctor rushed in, he didn´t know who to attend to first, because Javier was still lying where my father had left him, he did not look good at all, my uncle Julio, quickly took him out of his confused state...

"She is the one we called you for, leave that rabid dog alone."

"I can´t leave him like that sir, it is my duty to attend to him.

"Is he breathing?"

"Yes."

"Then the police will attend to him and you can treat him in prison, but not in this house."

As she heard his words, my mother looked up and said "Julio, let the doctor take a look at him, this should never have happened, Miguel should not have touched him."

My uncle looked at her, I could feel the controlled anger in his voice but I know he would never disrespect my mother.

"Carmen, if Miguel hadn´t put him in his place, one of us would have done so. Any man who beats up a woman is a coward and he needs to be made to feel the same pain. Rosario, how long has this been going on?"

I shook my head and turned away fixing my gaze on the opposite wall. Seconds later, the police arrived and the doctor informed them that I needed to be taken in to the hospital as I seemed to have fractured a few bones. Later when I was examined, my previous injuries were recorded and passed on to the detectives in charge of the case who questioned me, this time, I told them everything. Javier came to and was escorted from what till that moment had been our home, he was in handcuffs. Somebody must have alerted the press as they were waiting for him and the moment of his arrest was captured on film for all to see.

I return to the present and listen to the testimonies of my staff and those that witnessed the events of that fateful day, the photographs that Adela took of my previous injuries are also admitted as evidence and then I'm called to the stand to finally face my nemesis.

TWENTY-NINE

BALOU

I normally love being right, but this is the one time in my life I would have given anything to have been mistaken. However, like most animals I have the ability to discern evil when I come in contact with it. We read emotions and vibes much quicker than humans do and from the beginning I knew that there was just nothing good in that man, and everything he did or said was deceptive for a reason.

I´m not sure that if I had been human, it would have made much of a difference as Rosario would not have listened to me, she was a woman in love and when a woman is in that state, she defends the object of her affection with her life if necessary.

After Javier moved in, they seemed really happy but I still kept my distance from him because I simply did not like or trust him. I had heard Adela once say "When you dine with the devil, use a long spoon" and that is precisely what I intended to do. I watched him win over everybody, one by one, well to be fair, the women of the household. I wasn't sure that Juan and Marcos shared their enthusiasm but they kept their thoughts to themselves. It was true that I couldn't feel the tension in the air like when I first came to live with them, the atmosphere was much more relaxed. If Rosario was happy, then the only thing I could do was keep an eye on things.

However, a few days before the party, around the time her mother and brothers arrived, I noticed a subtle change in Javier's attitude and something else in his eyes, an emotion I couldn't quite place, so I decided to be on guard. I caught him looking at her in a way that sent shivers down my spine. I saw this a few times but in seconds his expression would change and he'd smile at her as if everything was perfect, sometimes I had to shake my head and look again just to see if I had imagined the whole thing. I began to fear for her especially because something told me that this time, it was different, I had a feeling that I couldn't shake off, something terrible was about to happen and I was determined to do my best to protect her but it was extremely unnerving not knowing when or how he was going to make his move. The only thing I was sure of was that he was going to do destroy something, it was that kind of dread you feel in the pit of your stomach and you just can´t get rid of.

As soon as her father arrived, my heart leapt for joy, the giant of a man came with his brothers that were also huge, I no longer felt alone or that it all depended on me, the army had landed.

I spent the whole day by his side while I kept my eyes on Javier and because I had succeeded in gaining his affections, he insisted I was sat by his side at the table, just as he had seen me sit on my stool in the kitchen, if this had not happened I would have been locked up with my friends and I don´t know what would have happened that night.

I jumped down from my stool after a most rewarding dinner in order to follow them all wherever they were going... From the corner of my eye I saw Marcos say something to Rosario, she excused herself and went up the stairs, then I noticed that a few seconds later, Javier followed on behind her.

It was the way he left the room, in such a furtive way, it made my heart pound, so I followed him... he entered the study and locked the door behind him, I rushed down the stairs quickly to carry out my plan.

I had been training my human grandfather all day and I hoped that now that I needed him, he would rise to the occasion and not fail me. I had taught him to run after me and try to catch me, we practised it a lot during the course of the day, he saw it as a game and laughed a lot as he ran after me, but in reality he was being prepared to get a job done. As I ran towards him I was hoping that he would be tempted to chase me and not ignore me because of all the guests that they were entertaining that night. I find people are well behaved when there are others present but this was the time to throw decorum aside.

I ran towards him and took a swipe at his leg and raced off, he laughed but turned to continue his conversation with the woman he was talking to, just as I feared he would do. It took three attempts for him to chase me, he put his glass down saying "Sorry, he won't stop till I get him, it's his favourite game" The woman laughed because the scene must have been funny if one was looking at it from a completely innocent point of view.

I ran past the study door and stopped just a bit after it just as he caught up with me, he was getting ready to let out a triumphant shout when we heard Rosario cry out and plead in anguish. Her father burst in to the room, the scene we found was horrifying. Rosario was on her knees while Javier was twisting her arm, which was by now in a very unnatural position behind her back. Her father quickly moved towards them, the noise he made as he did this was similar to that of a beast charging, in that split second before he hit him, Javier turned around to see what the noise was about, I saw something I had never seen in him before, fear.

In a matter of seconds he was on the floor and the older man was hitting him repeatedly, people started coming into the room and Rosario was quickly picked up by her aunt and her mother. I went towards her; I saw she had the same faraway and distant look she had when she used to stare for endless hours at the wall of her room. Someone closed the door so the guests remained outside, Carmen was screaming for her husband to stop, as he would kill him, I looked around and nobody moved, so she went towards him to try and stop him, but she was no match for him and called out to her son. Eventually with the help of another young man who strongly resembled the family, the three of them were able to tear them apart. She was crying while struggling with her husband, I could see in her, anger, compassion and fear. I could only see rage in Rosario´s father´s face, which had become a deep shade of red.

What surprised me most was the reaction of Javier´s parents. His father just stood there and watched while someone beat up his son, he even held his wife back so she couldn´t go and help him, her face had gone white and she

--

was crying and begging him to let her go. I still remember when Rosario told her that she could have prevented her from marrying her son; I wondered how she felt at that precise moment. I hoped she felt really guilty because like Miguel senior, I felt no pity towards that horrible man.

Her father was taken out of the room as soon as the police arrived. After Javier regained consciousness, he too was led out of the room, escorted by two uniformed men. I went down with them, I heard Javier's mother scream for them to arrest the man that had done that to her son, the police men stood for a moment looking quite uncertain as to how to proceed.

"We are not pressing any charges officers, our son attacked his daughter, the injuries he sustained were the result of trying to get him away from her" said Javier's father, his wife stood looking at him in surprise at the words she was hearing and was unable to react.

They put Javier in the back of the police car and I ran alongside it as it moved in the direction of the main gate, I had to make sure that he really left. Something told me that he would not be allowed back into the house this time.

The guests were kindly asked to leave and only the family remained behind, Rosario was taken to the hospital in an ambulance and her mother and two of her aunts went with her. Everyone was so shaken up and so quiet, I think I was the only happy one in the room, because despite all that had happened, for the first time, I no longer felt an evil presence in the house.

The staff were summoned... They were in shock at what had happened, they had been in the kitchen and only came out when they heard everybody rushing upstairs. Rosario's father was so nervous and furious, he kept pacing up and down the room.

"How long has this been going on?" He shouted.

The four of them looked down; I think they knew that their reply would not be liked.

"When I ask a question, I expect an answer."

" Señor we didn't find out for a long time and then she asked him to leave the house, he started getting treatment as it was discovered that he had a brain lesion, then months later, they got back together, we really did not have an opinion on anything that happened", replied Juan

"Are you saying that my daughter was living with a dangerous man who beat her up and not one of you thought to let her family know?"

"She ordered us not to tell anyone, even the doctor that came to treat her the last time..." Adela said; but she was quickly cut off by another shout. I have to say I admire that man, he has excellent lungs.

"Doctor? What doctor? Just start from the beginning as I´m losing my patience with you all."

They explained what had taken place while everyone listened in silence, after which Rosario´s father shouted at them for at least five minutes, in which he threatened their present jobs and the ability to ever get another one in the future, anywhere in the country. They were finally ordered in a not very polite manner to get out of his sight.

I went with them into the kitchen because, I knew that it was not the fault of my friends; their hands had been tied, just like my paws. They were just employees and in all honesty they had tried to get Rosario to go to the police and to go to the hospital. Both Adela and Marylin were crying, I rubbed myself against Adela´s legs to let her know that I didn´t agree with the horrible things that had been said to her and I felt myself being picked up from the floor and hugged tightly. You give some people a hand and they take the whole arm but I let it go, it was Adela.

"When two elephants fight, it is the grass underneath them that suffers", said Marcos, while all the staff stood in silence taking in his words.

Hours later when Rosario got back with her left arm in a sling, there was a lot more shouting from her father as they all listened to all that had happened over the past five years, there were a lot of tears from her mother who didn't understand how she could have suffered without saying a word to her family. After this, there was a silence and then Rosario got up and left the room, her mother after casting a reproachful look at the men in her family, went after her.

The next day we all left for Sevilla... I had thought that the mansion in Madrid was huge, but their ranch in the country made it look like a small apartment. There were lots of conversations and tears between mother and daughter, while I followed the father around the vast estate and grounds; he strode around angrily and muttering words of insult towards Javier and his entire family. Her parents had argued about his actions that day and Rosario's mother had made it clear that if he had gone to jail for killing Javier, he would have deserved it. She asked him what made him less a savage than their son-in-law, each time they argued about it, he would storm out with me closely by his side to show him my support. I loved being there, going to the stables where the magnificent horses he was so proud of were kept; going with him and the stable boys to let them out. He kept telling me that if it hadn't been for me, he had no idea what would have happened. There were reporters constantly at the gates, which are kilometres away from the house, each time someone came in or left the premises; they mentioned that they rushed towards the car to ask questions, microphones in hand.

We spent a few months there and I got to really live the dream of any cat, absolute freedom.

I heard them talk a lot about the court case, it seems Javier's mother has called a number of times to try to get Rosario to drop the charges but things are moving forward and justice is going to be served. Her lawyers spend a lot of time with her and prepare her for what will happen that day and all she will be asked. There is a special sadness in the house because a loved one has been suffering and the thought that she could have been killed is ever present in their conversations.

The day finally arrives when we have to go to Madrid for the case to be tried and we all leave solemnly. I hope they come back with the news that he is going to be locked away for the rest of his life.

JAVIER

Three years and six months. That is the jail sentence I was given for being a first time offender and because of the medical records my lawyers presented to the court to plead my case.

I look at Raquel Gónzalez, the prison psychiatrist while she takes down notes, I smile at her and she shyly smiles back. I know she finds me attractive and she has swallowed the story about my brain lesion, that I had no idea what I was doing and how it´s not my fault. She will be my ticket out of here for good behaviour. It´s amazing how even a professional, who is supposed to see red neon danger signs on my head, is oblivious to the fact that she is looking at a mask. It's a mask I put on to make people like me and believe what they see, something I´m really good at.

It is easier to accept that my accident made me this way and for them to feel sorry for me; the only one who saw through it all was that cat. When he looked at me he saw what I really was, someone who enjoyed inflicting pain on others and I knew that he knew. The way he stared at me...

Eva was not the first woman I hurt; I was just clever enough to hide my tracks very well on the previous occasions. After her, my parents kept a close eye on me and I was the perfect son for some time but I saw that whilst my father would not accept any other "incident", my mother on the other hand had defended and protected me with a passion, there were endless quarrels between them about me, but as I was apparently cured, after a while, nothing more was said. I became a model son, studied, got excellent grades and gave them no worries.

I met Rosario in USA; I had seen her previously on TV and in the press. Her family was extremely influential, the kind that was always at the top of the "Rich List", she was incredibly beautiful and self confident and I decided to destroy her as I did when I came in contact with anyone that had that special light in their eyes, the urge to extinguish it was just too much for me to resist. Despite her initial indifference, I set out to win her over and make her fall in love with me. This was not difficult for me as I´m an expert at being charming and giving people exactly what they want, this coupled with the fact that I'm not at all difficult to look at, got me her hand in marriage. I gave her a few months of happiness and security before I started systematically hurting her. I enjoyed seeing her puzzled look in the beginning, when she didn't understand what was going on, this turned to a look of fear before long.

She got depressed and would literally jump out of her skin each time I came into the room. I had her in the palm of my hands, if there is one thing that plays against celebrities, it is the mortal fear they have of people learning about their secrets... In my wife's case, her love for her family made her so much more vulnerable, she would rather die than let them know what she was going through.

I know my downfall is all thanks to that infernal cat. I did my best to make sure he didn't come into our house, I have never liked them. Cats just sit and watch you without wavering, like they can see your most secret intentions, I also hated that she loved him so much, I knew that it was him she centered all her affections on and even though I had hurt her so much, I wanted to be the most important thing in her life, I wanted her to feel all alone, isolated, with nothing to give her comfort. In other words, trapped.

After the staff found out what I had done, I did the only intelligent thing possible, I left the house and came back full of remorse, I met a stronger Rosario who was able to lay down the rules and that was when I resolved to win her back and this time, kill her. My accident was true, it was also true that I received a head injury but what was not true was that I didn't know what I was doing, but human beings like hearing and seeing what they want to. So I got the records, showed her, went to therapy and begged her to come to some of the sessions with me. I just sat down and invented feelings and past events which I knew would make her feel sorry for me.

I worked hard to gain back her trust and her love and eventually I was welcomed back into the house. I was the perfect husband and I saw her smile light up her eyes once again. I had her where I wanted her and I spent time imagining the best way to finish what I started.

I would have killed the cat, I did try to feed him treats laced with rat poison but he would have nothing to do with me and then I forgot about him to look at the bigger picture. That was the worst mistake I made as I now know that he was the one who led Rosario's father to the door. She had been so happy when her family came and I just couldn't resist the urge to punish her, her joy irritated me. My plan was for her to suffer a horrible accident a few days later, so I could move on. I was getting bored of playing the role of the perfect husband.

I know my father stood by and let me get beaten, I had actually not expected anything more from him. He came to the trial and testified that he was ashamed of me and what I did and he asked for the maximum sentence to be applied. How could he say that about his own son? I was hurt to hear his words and see his contempt towards me. My mother on the other hand was crying and asking the judge for mercy, she claimed I didn´t know what I was doing. I listened and marveled at her stupidity and gullibility and that she is afraid to stop and take a long, hard look at me.

I am going to be on my best behaviour here, when I get out, I´ll go to another country and lay low for a while before coming back to get Rosario and that cat. I do not like leaving loose ends.

EPILOGUE

I stand corrected; my parents have made it clear that they would have preferred me to have left Javier the very first time he raised his hand to me, than to have endured all those years in silence.

Now a year later, with my head clearer, the things I did out of fear seem really stupid. I look back and remember the look of sheer horror on the faces of my loved ones when they saw the Dantesque scene in front of them... I know that if I had done what I should have done in the beginning, I would have avoided that. Things can never be the same; there will always be a pain I can´t take away from any of us, which makes my whole sacrifice of keeping quiet completely useless.

Balou and I stayed with my parents for a few months after the trial but as each day passed, I knew what I had to do. I had to go back to Madrid and live my life. I had come to hate the city; it was the place where I had spent the worst years of my life. All that time, all I wanted to do was to get out of Madrid, return to where I had been so happy, where I felt the love and protection of my friends and family. I thought that I'd never ever want to return but I have discovered that I'm not the same Rosario that left Sevilla full of hopes and dreams just after my marriage. I got restless and little by little I realised that I had to go back to where I was most needed. I hadn't imagined that I would miss the people that had been by my side through it all, those who depended on me, people whom I loved and they loved me back. So once more, I packed my bags and Balou and I went back to Madrid.

I decide to do away with as many things as I can, things that remind me of the past. I put the house up for sale and buy another, one with a big garden for Balou to play in and for Adela to plant her vegetables and herbs in. The staff come with me, I learn about all the "lovely" things my father said to them. Throughout my absence I have paid their salaries as they are the people I trust and want them to remain by my side.

--

My marriage is in the process of being annulled on the grounds of extreme cruelty and a number of other factors. Padre Antonio says I argue less and less with him each time about "coming home" and I tell him that when I read about a death due to domestic violence, I feel like my life was saved because someone was sent to watch over me. If that is true, I have no desire to argue or be ungrateful.

I have come to realise that when things happen, everyone tells you what you should have done, sometimes even with impatience! We all urge the victims of domestic abuse to leave and go to the police, but words are only too easy to utter for those who are not going through what you are. It is an extremely complicated situation where a lot of feelings and personal circumstances play a very important part in making the wrong decision of allowing someone to break them down. I have seen what my silence did to the people that love me, I can't imagine what my death would have done to them. I need to be able to use my story to get the message through to them; it never gets better once the cycle starts.

That day outside the court house, I saw the women that the Foundation is helping, standing in silence showing their support, standing by their side was Eva, she smiled at me and I knew that she understood what I had gone through. No matter how long I took to heal, I had to come back because now that my secret was out, I had to be an example to others and help them in any way I could. The worst was finally over, at least for me.

I did not want to go into the pet shop that day, I did not want an animal but the moment Balou and I locked eyes, I knew that I was no longer alone. Now it's time to write the next chapter of our lives.

TO BE CONTINUED....

ACKNOWLEDGEMENTS

I would like to express my profound gratitude to practically everyone I know. In a bigger or smaller way you have all contributed to this book seeing the light of day. I feel incredibly lucky to have people in my life who constantly encourage me to pursue my dreams.

¡Muchas gracias!

Printed in Great Britain
by Amazon.co.uk, Ltd.,
Marston Gate.